CHEAP THERAPIST SAYS YOU'RE INSANE

STORIES

Parker Young

Future Tense Books

Portland, Oregon

ISBN: 978-1-892061-95-9

Edited by Kevin Sampsell and Emma Alden.
Layout by Michael Kazepis.
Cover design by Emma Alden.
Cover art by Minami Kobayashi, *In the Bath Room*, Oil on canvas.

First edition. Printed in the United States of America.

Published by Future Tense Books. Portland, Oregon

www.futuretensebooks.com

Contents

Golden Hour	13
Collaboration	18
On the Toilet	24
Carbon Monoxide	32
Surveillance	44
Oven Blew Up	56
Myrtle Beach	58
Sleeplessness	64
(911)	71
Opera Singer	73
Flight to Paradise	75
Steady Work	80
Repentance Rebate	86
Disappearances	93
May 24	102

Writing Fiction 106

Lance, LeBron, Sam, and Polly 109

Letters Become Bricks 123

Chicken Marriage Sandwich 127

Two Bathtubs in Memphis 130

My Idea for a Building Plus One Joke 138

Van Gogh at Work 141

Cheap Therapist Says You're Insane 145

RIP Bobby 148

Man Against Mansion 150

Armchair 151

Missing Person 154

Shivering in Virginia 158

3:30 162

Realistic Outcomes 165

My Shoes 168

FLO-RITE 170

The Story Behind the Stories 173

There are melodies that we never hear for the first time. What I mean is that we've been hearing them since before we learned to speak.

—Luis Sagasti

Golden Hour

I was walking around my neighborhood from block to block, trying to think, trying to figure out why everyone hated me, or why I felt that to be the case at least, getting nowhere, when I realized I was being followed. From a distance, he looked exactly like me. I tried to ignore this.

What else happened? I saw a woman in her living room, pacing with a knife. This was late evening, when sunlight fades enough to make peering through windows easy, before people remember to let down the blinds. The golden hour, or just past the golden hour. She's beautiful, I thought, but it could have been the false intimacy of seeing her at home, alone, pacing with a knife.

She shouldn't be pacing with a knife, I thought, it won't lead to anything good.

Then I remembered the man following behind me. I began to worry. It's fine to see one strange thing on a neighborhood walk, but two suggests a pattern, and every pattern has a source. The source was either me (insanity) or God (Hell is real).

I walked faster. I tried to calm myself by saying, The odds of a third thing are infinitesimal. I said infinitesimal aloud, practically jogging now, thinking about the knife, saying infinitesimal. The knife was in the living room with the woman. It should have been in the kitchen. She shouldn't have been pacing. A walk around the neighborhood is just like pacing. But I didn't have a knife. Which was now part of the problem.

Then I heard the man behind me cough or spit or sneeze or something, and I tried to go faster but couldn't—this was my top walking speed. I'll just go home, I thought. But home was exactly what I needed to avoid, because I couldn't do my best thinking there. I needed to walk, I needed to think, and what I needed to think about was why everyone hated me, or else why I thought everyone hated me. In some cases, the two can converge: you become convinced everyone hates you, which alters your behavior in insipid ways, causing you to fight false battles, giving everyone good reason to hate you.

The man following me dropped something, and I tried to pretend it was something else, but I knew it was a knife. They both have knives, I thought, that's three strange things, the pattern continues unabated. Everyone had a knife but me. I didn't even have a good knife at home—nothing but butter knives and a now-dull family heirloom, a paring knife. I could remember my grandfather using it to peel tomatoes. With terror, I realized I'd never peeled a tomato. I decided to return to the pacing woman's house for protection. She had a good knife, by the look of it. Maybe she would protect me from the man behind, who was closing in.

He's not me, I told myself, referring to the man behind, even if he looks like it. He's not my brother either. I don't have a brother. It must be harder to go insane if you have a brother—I'd like to see the figures on that.

It was possible, of course, that everyone was really and truly mad at me for some good, unassailable reason.

By the time I circled back to the woman's apartment, she had let down the blinds. I knocked on the door. What if it's the wrong apartment? I thought. But the man behind was closing in, so it didn't matter. I knocked again while the man behind drew closer. The door cracked open.

Yes, said the woman.

I knew it would be her! But I hadn't thought of what to say.

Can I borrow your knife? I said.

My life? she said.

No, your knife, I said.

Well, no, she said, and she tried to slam the door shut, but I couldn't let her do that, on account of the man behind, who was closing in, so I wedged my foot between the door and doorframe. She shouted, but not a wordless shout. Her shout formed a sentence: Lenny, come help. I almost smiled, because I already knew something about this man, Lenny, who lived with her. She wanted to stab him. That's why she'd been pacing with a knife. Now she wanted to stab me. Or she wanted him to stab me. Maybe Lenny had the knife now; they could have been taking turns with the knife, each thinking secretly of stabbing the other, pacing, muttering, envisioning step-by-step how it would go, the stabbing, disposal of the body, etc., until I had arrived, suggesting by my very presence a miraculous new means of salvaging their relationship. They would stab me instead. Now they were a team again, the woman and Lenny, united in their effort to stab me. But I wanted them to stab the man behind me (if they could tell us apart).

Now the real question was, what would Lenny do? How fast was he? Was he sitting or standing when the woman called his name? And could he handle a knife? It was all relevant because the man behind was closing in.

Lenny, I screamed, hoping to confuse him into joining my cause, at least for a moment. Sometimes a moment is all it takes. The crucial moment. I couldn't remove my foot because the woman was still leaning against the door. The man behind was closing in. I pushed against the door with all my weight, creating just enough space to extract my foot as the door slammed shut.

I turned and shuffled quickly down the sidewalk, trying to think, trying to figure out why everyone hated me. I knew I was being foll

.

Collaboration

I was writing a fantastic tale about two little sheep who have nowhere to go but up. The main question that animates the story is, will the sheep go up? It seems they should—they have no reason not to. Certainly, they can't go any further down. We all have limits.

Anyway, that was the story I was writing, and the writing was going well until my wife began changing the words of the story at night, when I wasn't looking. I've got no proof, of course, it's only a feeling I have, but a strong one. For example, one of the two sheep is now a female sheep. I can't remember writing a female sheep into the story, but there it is, and its name is Tina. On the other hand, I was never dead set on writing a story about two male sheep, so I guess it's possible that I was the one who made one sheep male and the other sheep female and named the female one Tina. There's nothing wrong with a sheep named Tina, and I would never claim otherwise. But in this case, it's suspicious, because my wife's name is Tina and my name is Colin, and can you guess what the male sheep's name is?

I think I should ask Tina what's going on.

———

A new development. The sheep are no longer sheep—now they are people. People who walk upright and spend lots of time watching tennis. This is troubling because I would never write about tennis. I love to watch tennis myself and have spent a large portion of my life doing so, but I would never go so far as to write it into a story of mine, especially not a story about two people like Colin and Tina. Yes, I'm a tennis-watching type of person through and through, but I'm determined to hide such proclivities from the world for as long as possible, so I can't help but suspect that my wife is interfering with my story and changing the words all around at night, when I'm not looking. This is a serious charge because I hardly ever sleep. Therefore, in order for her to change the words of my story all around, she would have to spend hours pretending to sleep, waiting attentively for the precise moment when I've actually drifted off for my forty-five minutes or so. Then and only then would she be able to strike, affecting change in my story about Colin and Tina, who used to be sheep and had nowhere to go but up. Writing about the time they spend watching professional tennis, which I would never, ever do. The writing about it, that is.

I think I should ask Tina what's going on.

———

The final straw. The Colin character has disappeared completely from my story, which is now a Tina story about Tina things. Tina alone in restaurants, Tina alone on the train, Tina, who used to be a sheep with nowhere to go but up, watching professional tennis and drinking too much. It's my personal opinion that in the story she drinks too much, but the arc of the narrative never seems to suggest that her drinking is a problem. A real problem. But a problem that has nothing to do with the story's original question, which was, these sheep who have nowhere to go but up, will they go up? Or not? It seems they should.

Maybe I'll delete it. After all, I can't handle reading any more about Tina, especially if she's going to go on drinking gin and watching tennis for god knows how many more pages. Making eyes at strangers.

Tina, I say, can I ask you something?

But she's drunk. Tina rarely drinks, and so it only takes an hour or two out with friends to render her inoperable. I'll have to ask later.

———

Tina, I say over breakfast, have you been using my laptop?

No, she says.

Tina, I say later, what are you pouring into your coffee?

Cream, she says.

Irish cream?

Normal cream. Would you like some?

No thank you, I say.

You're too masculine for cream.

That's right.

Well, thanks for making breakfast, she says. Should we go for a walk?

Sorry, I say, opening my laptop. I've got too much to do.

———

I have no choice now but to delete the story, which features a new character named Anticolin who wears a beautiful camelhair jacket. Anticolin owns his own small business. He watches professional tennis proudly, somehow ostentatiously, in fact he's a dandy in terms of paying attention to professional tennis, he's a complete clotheshorse for tennis-watching. I guess it goes without saying that he barely understands the sport at all. Basically, he's a lunatic. But nobody in the story seems to care. They're all happy to have Anticolin around, watching tennis at the bar, buying drinks for everyone else with his company credit card. Moving happily, carelessly through the story, which is ostensibly my story, with Tina, my wife, watching tennis in all the trendiest places to be seen watching tennis across town.

———

I'm alone, sitting on the couch, making a deliberate effort not to think about the sheep or Tina or Colin or Anticolin or anything else from the story I've just deleted, when Tina, the real Tina, sits beside me and asks if I've seen any good tennis recently.

No, I say. It's not good for me.

I disagree, she says. I think it has a rejuvenating effect.

I prefer not to watch it, I say, although the truth is that the first thing I do whenever she leaves the house is turn on tennis.

Now that she's mentioned it, it's all I can think about, tennis, which must have been her intended effect exactly. That's when I realize she's still trying to change the story I was writing. After all, the story still exists in my head. I can't delete it there.

———

I was never able to answer the story's main question, which was, in a world where going up can mean the same thing as going down, will the sheep go up? In other words, will they persevere? Despite knowing that their perseverance is meaningless?

Tina, I say, can I ask you something?

Hmmm? she says.

Why do you persevere?

Are you asking me why people persevere in general?

No. You, personally.

Simple, she says. Because I love you.

On the Toilet

On November 12, 2015, in a tweet punctuated by four exclamation marks, Stephen Curry announced that his wife had bought him an automatic toilet.

Curry, one month later in an interview with ESPN: I bet if I did a case study on my performance since I got the toilet, you'd see the difference.

Six months later, the Warriors became the first team in basketball history to blow a 3-1 series lead in the NBA Finals.

I wasn't doing well that summer, but I'd rather not say why.

In 2014, toilet-maker Flushmate recalled its line of high-pressure toilets due to multiple explosions. For many years, I feared that a poisonous spider hiding in a toilet would bite me fatally in the ass.

ESPN: Were you on the new pot when you posted that tweet?
Curry: Well, I am a big social-media-on-the-toilet guy, because that's my break time. But no, I was in Minnesota… And the next day I had 46 [points]. There's a reason for that. I was very happy.

Everyone knows Elvis died on the toilet.

One of my favorite scenes in literature, from Kobo Abe's *The Ark Sakura*, involves the protagonist of the novel getting his foot stuck in an unusually high-powered toilet.

Judy Garland died on the toilet.

I have never had sex on a toilet.

I have never, as far as I can recall, fallen into a toilet.

John Harrington probably invented the first flush toilet in 1596, but his invention failed to catch on with society at large due to the terrible stench it introduced to the home.

Around the same time, Harrington completed the first English translation of the epic Italian poem *Orlando Furioso*.

The author of *Orlando Furioso* spent 26 years writing and revising it. According to the novelist David Markson.

Man proposes, God disposes, is a quote widely misattributed to Ludovico Ariosto, the author of *Orlando Furioso*.

Flush toilets were not widely adopted until the late 18th century, when Alexander Cummings designed the S-shaped pipe which prevents the sewage smell from rising into the home.

Cummings is buried in Joseph Grimaldi park, where Joseph Grimaldi, the famous English clown, is also buried.

In 1832, the clown Grimaldi and his wife, Mary, made a suicide pact. However, the poison they used was faulty and led to nothing more than acute indigestion.

Their failed suicide proved so traumatic that they could never bring themselves to try suicide again.

The one experience I shall never describe, Virginia Woolf called her intended suicide. According to Markson.

I recommend installing a bidet.

I have never flushed anything valuable down the toilet. Drugs for example.

The comedian Lenny Bruce died on the toilet.

I was once forced to ask my mother-in-law for help locating her plunger.

It's in the garage.

Once, while working on a movie in Atlanta, the bathroom I was using began to move. The teamster driving the restroom trailer had decided to change locations.

A few days later, I met another teamster named Earl who claimed to be the drummer in Bad Brains.

We were working on a Christmas comedy which features one of Robin Williams' final performances.

The movie didn't turn out well. The screenwriter asked to have his credit vacated. The official credit now belongs to a fictitious Michael Brown.

The movie includes a car chase scene which climaxes when a porta-potty is intentionally dropped off the back of a truck, wrecking a pursuing state trooper, Mario Kart-style.

The most famous toilet fatality in cinema is probably in *Pulp Fiction*.

My wife says there is also a toilet fatality in *Jurassic Park*, although I've never seen it.

Just before filming on the Christmas comedy began, I ate dinner at the same table as Joel McHale. He made fun of me for ordering fish.

Further down the same table, I overheard Tim Heidecker discussing Terrence Mallick's movie *The Tree of Life* in reverent tones.

Seven years later, I read an article in *The Believer*, an interview with Heidecker in which he mentions *The Tree of Life* again.

Later in that same interview: Gregg [Turkington] and I have this thing going where we pretend to be two guys talking who aren't super familiar with toilets. Like, 'You know, the thing with the bowl, it's a round... pot.' 'Oh yes, I know what you mean.' It kills us.

In 336 AD, the heretic Arius died on the toilet. His death was widely believed to be a form of divine retribution.

Arianism (not to be confused with the racial dogma of Aryanism) suggests that Jesus is not God the Father's equal but his subordinate.

Many historians now believe Arius was poisoned by opponents of his theology.

Treason doth never prosper; what's the reason?
For if it prosper, none dare call it treason.
    —John Harrington, inventor of the flush toilet

Does toilet water actually spin in opposite directions on opposite sides of the equator?

If a toilet is installed on the equator, which way will its water spin?

Could this be a viable means of determining the exact location of the equator?

Idea for an art installation: a toilet on rails which can slide to either side of the equator, allowing users to determine which way the water spins on the way down.

The installation could be called *Earth's Only Natural Border*.

Due to subtle polar movement in the earth's rotation, the *true equatorial plane* drifts about 30 feet throughout the year.

Therefore, the exhibit itself would also need to be on rails.

My two-year-old sometimes flips sentences so that the object acts upon the subject.

The rubber ducky has Ernie.

The toilet is on Daddy.

My poop is afraid of me.

Stephen Curry recently won his fourth NBA championship.

When I told my therapist about Curry's automatic toilet, he said, There's a guy who wants nothing to do with his own shit.

Carbon Monoxide

Just to get out of the apartment on my days off, I sometimes visited some friends of mine who ran a cactus store on Echo Park Avenue. I lived nearby, my apartment building adjacent on both sides to the homes of retirement-age couples, terrific friends apparently, always inviting each other over for dinner, and as a result it had become impossible to determine who lived in which building. Maybe they had abandoned such formalities. At night I saw their silhouettes make abbreviated gestures into the street, levitating beer cans. They seemed pleased to ignore me.

Anyway, Paul and Kathryn ran the cactus store. Ran is a generous word. They locked and unlocked the doors in an unpredictable pattern. I can't remember if I ever saw a customer. Maybe I was their only customer—once I bought a cactus for no other reason than I liked the word: cactus. Then I forgot to take it home. Maybe other people bought it later too. We liked to sit together in the back of their store and drink beer.

One day, instead of beginning in the back of the store, we met at a bar in Atwater Village. I'd never heard of this bar before. I don't know who suggested it or why. I do recall that once we got there, we seemed to be waiting for some important person to arrive, an icon of culture. They wouldn't tell me who it was.

Willie Nelson? I guessed.

Who? said Kathryn. No.

Do I know this person?

You'll be filled with awe and gratitude, she said, I'm warning you.

I smelled a gas leak which I declined to mention. It was an old bar. I thought, maybe what I smell is its age. My tallboy grew slippery in my hand. Soft-rock played, causing all my thoughts to become soft-rock-themed. It's hard to think that way. I suggested, at the very start, that we find a new bar on account of the soft rock music, but Paul and Kathryn ignored me. They didn't even respond to my suggestion, it made so little sense to them. In conclusion, they probably couldn't hear the music because their thoughts were soft-rock-themed already. They had a permanent soft rock sensation in their minds, which meant that whenever they encountered soft rock music in the world, they felt properly aligned. They filled up with a perverse kind of clarity.

The only downside is I didn't lose any weight, said Paul. He was talking about surviving cancer.

Kathryn said, I heard they studied mice with cancer and found that the mice, on average, lived longer after the initial diagnosis than humans with similar kinds of cancer. Even though the humans received medical treatment and the mice did not.

Wow.

Yes. They attributed the difference to the mouse's superior cancer-fighting mindset.

Mice don't want to die. They never have, said Paul.

I'd put my money on you, Paul, I said, over any sort of cancerous rodent.

That's kind of you.

If I may comment objectively, said Kathryn, I think you're at a disadvantage because you know that death is inevitable. It takes some of the wildness out of you. But it makes you cunning.

Paul said, I already beat the mice anyway through the power of modern surgery and anesthesiology. They cut the problem right out.

How did it feel? I asked.

Like nothing. I don't think I even dreamed while I was under. Paul shrugged.

This beer was making me float already. It opened me up. When it opened me up, more soft rock got in, I noticed. An example of a soft rock thought: the sudden urge to gush to your friend about a poem you've never read. My heart rate quickened. I wondered if I should mention the gas leak. I couldn't smell it anymore, which was either a good sign or a bad sign, I didn't know which.

Beer is almost as good as anesthesiology. And way cheaper, said Paul.

Now I couldn't remember if we were actually waiting for someone important to appear, or if that was a joke. The bartender took away Paul's empty can and supplied a fresh one. I'd lost track of how many he'd had. That's the principal advantage of drinking in a bar. The bartender expunges the record after each drink. The evidence is disposed of. You don't have to find a trash can or make any movement at all. Every drink is the first and only drink. Until the check comes. And maybe, if you're in the kind of money the two of them seemed to be in (where did it come from?), not even then.

I had an aunt who was a famous anesthesiologist, I said.

I hear that one a lot, said Paul.

Well, she wasn't really famous. But she put a few famous people under.

Who?

Richard Nixon. I forget who else.

I don't believe you, said Kathryn.

Personally, I can't believe Nixon would survive surgery, said Paul. He wasn't well-liked in his time.

At one point, he was popular enough to become the president.

Paul said, Actually, I think I would be a decent president. I make difficult decisions with surpassing ease. A shocking amount of ease, some might say.

What are you talking about? said Kathryn.

For example, I once hit a deer with my car simply because I had a premonition that the driver behind me, an elderly woman, would hit it. Time slowed. I could see her bobbed grey hair and trembling fingers. I've got a better chance of surviving, I decided, so I changed my trajectory in order to make impact. I altered the fate of everyone involved. Except the deer, I guess.

I remember that differently, said Kathryn.

That's because you were thrown from the car and lost consciousness for hours, said Paul.

They say a pine tree saved my life, said Kathryn.

Anyway, surgeons don't kill people they dislike, I said. It's unprofessional.

That may be true. But I worked hard to make sure my surgeons liked me. You can't convince me it didn't pay off.

I think my aunt would have done a good job on Hitler.

Don't say that name too loud in here. You'll attract the wrong crowd, said Paul.

Really? Kathryn and I said at once.

I'm kidding. These people are nice. Although I did meet a Nazi here once.

How did you know?

We were having a normal conversation about tennis. Then he said to me, Ever seen Germany's World War II uniforms? You got to admit it: they were pretty cool. And he looked at me with a look that could be labeled Invitation to the Brotherhood, you know. It was scary.

What did you say?

Nothing. I said nothing. I just disengaged.

I put my phone away. I had been trying and failing to find my aunt's name in an article about Richard Nixon's surgery for phlebitis, an inflammation of the blood vein. The surgery didn't really go well. His stomach grew dangerously full of fluids. Nixon lost a lot of blood. I found an unnerving typo in a 1974 *New York Times* article about the surgery. It referred to part of the procedure as the replacement blood kiss. Elsewhere, it referred to the replacement blood lass. Blood kisses and blood lasses. A confusion of blood and tenderness. And the President trying not to die.

I leaned into Kathryn's ear to whisper, I think there's a gas leak.

What's this? demanded Paul. Secrets?

Hm, said Kathryn.

I just said I think there's a gas leak.

They don't use gas here. Troy? Do you use gas here? Paul asked the bartender.

No, said Troy the bartender. We never use it.

This is a gas-free environment, said Paul.

Later, his head stopped moving. It was just angled over his beer. I worried his neck would give way and the glass nozzle would give him a shiner.

I called for Troy.

Where's the carbon monoxide detector?

Right here. He pointed at his nose. Beep! he said.

What does beep mean? I asked, growing sick.

One beep is good. Two is bad, he said

He poured us apple pie shots for no reason and wiped the counter. Three apple pie shots. Then I understood. This was a Wisconsin-themed bar. Packers merchandise on the walls. All my life, I've responded to Packers merchandise with revulsion. I don't know why. The color scheme offends me somehow. A shameless combination of forest green and cheddar yellow. It's a cynical way to reckon with the world, smashing green and yellow together that way. The music had shifted from soft rock to intolerable soft jazz. Troy the bartender wore what appeared to be a hat in support of the president. He must have just put it on. I would have noticed it before. I averted my gaze. Troy beeped again. I looked away from everything, just to steady myself, down into the corner of the room, but there I saw an unlidded cooler full to overflowing with—I couldn't believe it—rifle ammunition. Did they chill the bullets and drop them into drinks? I inspected mine closely.

When I looked back, Paul seemed to be crying.

I voted for Hillary, he said to nobody in particular. Just so you know.

———

Our evening should have stopped there. I should have canceled everything. Instead, I made the mistake of going back to their cactus shop to help with a six pack. We began discussing dreams. Paul told us about a dream of his in which a revolutionary war was taking place within the charred remains of our city. His mission as a member of the resistance, he told us, was to throw a very special exploding brick through a certain residential window in the Mid-Wilshire neighborhood. But in the middle of his journey to the window, he found himself under considerable pressure to make people laugh, and so he ate the brick. After that, he didn't know what to do. He couldn't by any means continue his mission now that the brick was gone. The dream continued with an episode in a museum full of disappeared paintings, but that part wasn't very interesting. I only mention it because it reminded me to tell the story about the paint-and-sip class.

The paint-and-sip class was an absurd BYOB networking event for aspiring film editors. I can't remember how I convinced myself to go. I brought a bottle of red wine which I poured continually into a little plastic cup. Most people drank beer and hid behind the little pieces of canvas they were supposed to be transforming. Not much networking occurred, really. The painting selected for us to emulate was Cape Cod Evening, a Depression-era work by Edward Hopper. In the painting, man and wife lounge hungrily before their home while daylight vanishes and their dog, an attentive border collie, listens closely to the sounds of the forest just beyond. Everything is lit drastically, like a scene from the end of an unhappy play. Our instructor stood in front, watching us drink, explaining simple brush-stroke techniques which he claimed would lead us straight into the realm of Edward Hopper. He told us over and over not to be afraid. Be bold, he said, make it your own. Do not be afraid. After an hour and most of a bottle of wine, I noticed that something unusual had occurred on my canvas—the dog was bleeding. I applied more paint in an effort to heal the dog. But the bleeding only grew worse. I didn't know what to say. When the instructor looked over my shoulder, he nodded thoughtfully and smiled in assurance.

Help me, I said.

No, said the instructor, I won't consider it. You've got a nice touch.

You know, we have a strange dog in real life, said Kathryn.

Oh, that, said Paul, Jesus.

Does it bleed for no reason? I said.

No, but it poops. Like, forty times a day.

Wow, I said.

It is truly a magical dog.

We're lucky to have such a big yard.

She can't help it.

What's her name? I said.

Georgeanne.

Georgeanne, I thought, stunned.

Want to know how I would help your dog? I said. Then I made a hand gesture involving a gun.

Together they stood.

Okay, don't hurt me, I said.

I began to back deliberately down the hall, one step at a time, away from the back office, into the storefront, while they followed at exactly the same pace, Paul rapping his knuckles against the wall. I'll kill you, he said. Something was wrong with them, they had been snagged in tandem by the same quickening dream, and it was my fault, or maybe my hand's fault—I was now convinced my hand had caused all this trouble by making such a convincing gun. There's always some latent violence in the fingers of people, in the very shape of them, waiting for a chance to emerge, the simplest transformation. I'll break your arm off, said Kathryn as we continued our march. A few paces from the door, I noticed the potted cactus I had paid money for months ago and never taken home. Had it always been so beautiful? Three purple flowers hovered like music above the white needles and green flesh.

My cactus, I said, grabbing it by the red clay pot.

No, said Kathryn.

No, I paid! Remember?

No! You paid for that one, she said, pointing to a gnarled, collapsed specimen.

I clutched my flowering cactus, the one I had paid for, as near to my heart as possible.

How do you make money? I said. I've never understood it.

Outside, the sun touched every part of the sky. I cranked my Honda Accord and drove down Echo Park Avenue, caught the green light at Sunset Boulevard and sailed straight through the intersection, feeling like a local. This was my neighborhood, my home. At my side, my cactus, a trustworthy associate. I knew where we were going and where street parking might be available. Sure enough, a stretch of naked curb appeared by the sign that welcomes people to the park, across the street from a stucco church building of obscure denomination. I've heard of church doors that don't have locks, but this church was different. Its doors didn't have hinges. Its doors couldn't do the job of a door. Which meant they weren't doors at all. Nothing happens when people knock.

Surveillance

They tried to talk about my brother on the news, but they didn't know what happened. He may have robbed a jewelry store, they said, but the problem was, no jewelry was missing. Furthermore, my brother hasn't left the store. He's still in there. Maybe that's why the jewelry can't yet be considered missing. My brother, even as I write this, stands inside the store, head bowed over a display case—that much is well-documented. He is wearing a jacket. Everyone wants to know what's inside the jacket. If I knew, I would tell you. I hope it's nothing unusual—just the normal things people keep in jackets.

The question is, if jewels are inside his jacket (and we can't prove they are), does that constitute theft? Remember that he hasn't yet left the store's premises.

Even if he does exit the store with jewelry inside his jacket, I've been told that he's allowed to walk ten feet past the door. This provision exists in case he's a smoker. I don't think he smokes. Still, I'm glad the provision exists.

———

If (and that's a big if) he has jewelry in his jacket, what kind of jewelry is it? Something that might belong in a jacket, like a pocket watch? In that case, what could be more natural than to pocket the pocket watch before purchase, just to see how it feels? If, on the other hand, a diamond ring or necklace is inside the jacket, that would be harder to defend. Although it's true that my brother has been dating a woman for over a year. Maybe he's preparing to propose. Maybe he wants to see how the ring feels in his pocket. Unfortunately, nobody likes his girlfriend, so this is probably the least likely scenario of all. If my brother had a nice girlfriend, in other words, he'd have a legitimate reason to temporarily put an unpurchased ring in his jacket. But he doesn't.

I hope nothing is in there.

―――――

My brother has been standing in the store for hours. Nobody knows if he's a thief or a customer. We're all waiting to find out. The local news films from every angle. He appears calm. Law enforcement has established a secure perimeter while maintaining a low profile.

A watchmaker sits behind a nearby display case as if nothing is happening, polishing watches. His shift ends in an hour, I've been told.

I'll visit my brother soon and drop off a letter of encouragement.

It's all streaming online at this point.

It seems possible that he's forgotten whether or not he has anything in his jacket.

―――――

We must consider the pants. In my opinion, the jacket has been excessively scrutinized. It's only fair to give the pants some thought. The pants have at least four pockets: two in front, two in back. There may be a very small fifth pocket inside one of the larger front pockets. Nobody uses the fifth pocket, but we must give everything thorough consideration. That's how my brother will be exonerated: thorough consideration. Unless that's how he'll be indicted. Which he won't be. Although to be honest, I fear the worst.

I see the outline of a small object in his front right-hand pants pocket. It could be keys or a wallet or a phone. Actually, he has two phones. The second phone is for his second girlfriend. Everyone likes her much more than his first girlfriend. We all—my other brother and our mutual friends—bemoan the fact that she's been assigned the second phone. And now his poor judgment will cost him, because if his second girlfriend were in the first phone, per our unanimous request, it would be more plausible for my brother to have a diamond ring in his jacket (or pants) pocket (although he probably doesn't). In that case, people might believe that he was testing the ring to see how it felt in his jacket (or pants), simulating the hours before the proposal, as it's prudent to do. Conversely, nobody would believe he's planning to propose to his first girlfriend. And it's equally hard to believe he would propose to a woman relegated to the second phone, no matter how attractive she might be. Because if he likes her so much, why isn't she in the first phone? What a disaster.

———

After careful study, I now believe the object protruding from his pants pocket is a keychain.

I'm reminded now of my old coworker, Howard. He kept a diamond ring on his keychain. I asked him why. He said it was his wife's request—apparently, wearing the ring caused her unbearable anxiety, so she asked Howard to safeguard it. Later, I decided to introduce myself to her at the company holiday party; I broached the topic right away, summing up everything my coworker Howard had told me already. Listen, I said to her, if you don't mind me asking, why don't you trust yourself to wear it?

I pointed at her ring finger. Then I looked over at Howard. His face all mashed in.

The woman said, You're married?

Well, said Howard.

Now I regret my reluctance to ask Howard some follow-up questions. Howard, my colleague, whose job was to redact security footage of public masturbators in the park. Maybe he had a good reason for the ring on his keychain. I lacked the courage to ask. Maybe my brother is in an analogous situation, a Howard sort of situation. If jewelry is found on his keychain (and I'm not suggesting it will be), I wish I could say to the authorities, Listen, there's a precedent for this sort of behavior. Then I could tell the story of Howard.

But without the full story, my information will be considered trivial. If I simply give the fragmented account of Howard presented above, a story without any explanation, they'll assume Howard obtained his diamond ring illegally as well. They'll bug his phone line. I wonder how many phones Howard has. I'd have to tell him to stop using them all.

———

My brother peed his pants. It was bound to happen—the jewelry store has no restroom for customers. The footage is gaining traction online. The livestream audience grows and grows. Views approaching the hundreds of millions for my brother, who has either stolen jewelry or is stealing jewelry or has never even begun the process of stealing jewelry. It's possible he's never even begun the *thought process* of stealing jewelry and has no idea why all the cameras and policemen are responding so sensitively to his presence. Maybe he just wanted one of those free cups of coffee the store offers to browsing customers.

Wait… because of the coffee, shouldn't there be a bathroom available on the premises? That's a state law.

It's possible that upon realizing he was in a space which failed to comply with state bathroom laws, my brother was paralyzed by fear. If you have a fear of not finding a bathroom where one ought to be (as clearly delineated by state law), and if that fear affects you to such a high degree that it becomes physically paralyzing, it becomes a self-realizing fear. The threat which the fear detects is, by virtue of the body's reaction to the fear, an unstoppable promise, a premonition. The threat becomes reality. Unless someone intervenes. Which, admittedly, I have not done.

———

It's not against any law I know of to stand or to pee your pants in a jewelry store which serves free coffee downtown while a watchmaker stands nearby, polishing watches. With millions of people watching and re-watching across every platform of social media. With your brother at home on the couch, trying and failing not to watch.

———

They confiscated the jacket. They had no right to do it, but predictably they did. This is how the end begins. Fortunately, nothing of value was inside. Just a granola bar and a phone.

The phone could be either the first phone or the second phone. It's impossible to know without unlocking it. If it's his second phone, that means his second phone is now his first phone. I believe that's how it works. And so I hope, for reasons I already quite clearly explained, that it's the phone I think of as the second phone.

———

Too late to worry about the phone. The authorities are now preparing—I don't know why—to destroy it in a controlled explosion.

I involuntarily touch my own phone in my pocket to make sure it's still there.

His phone explodes. The smoke settles in the demolition tent, which has its own live stream online. Applause follows.

The t-shirt my brother is wearing doesn't have any pockets.

Now it's just his pants.

Maybe that's why he peed his pants: in order to confuse our thinking regarding the pants.

I hope that's not true. If he felt the need to confuse our pants-related thought process, that means there's probably jewelry in the pants. Unless it's in his socks or shoes.

Which is not to say that I actually think he has jewelry in his socks or shoes.

He may not even be wearing socks. You can put any kind of cloth between your shoes and your feet.

It could be a prayer cloth, for example.

I hope he uses prayer cloths instead of socks. That might win him some points at trial. If there is a trial. Which would be outrageous.

─────

The police have slowly, almost imperceptibly, begun to tighten their circle around my brother.

─────

The watchmaker I mentioned who was polishing watches days ago—he never left. He simply removed his sweater and slacks to reveal, beneath it all, a police uniform. He's a part-time watchmaker, part-time policeman. But maybe that's a lucky break for my brother. This man probably thinks more like a policeman than a watchmaker when he's on the clock for the jewelry store, and more like a watchmaker than a policeman when he's on the clock for the police. A man who secretly thinks like a police officer when you expect him to be thinking like a watchmaker is twice as dangerous as an obvious police officer. In other words, now that the watchmaker has stopped thinking secret police officer thoughts and, by becoming a police officer, begun secretly to think like a watchmaker, my brother is at a slightly smaller disadvantage than before. A policeman-watchmaker is the worst kind of watchmaker. But not the worst kind of policeman.

———

There's a new rumor going around which suggests that the reason my brother hasn't pooped yet is he swallowed the jewelry. They're saying he doesn't want the jewelry to pass through his digestive system. This rumor spread so quickly that they now have a camera solely dedicated to monitoring the situation with his ass. It's a special camera, algorithmically equipped to monitor changes in density and volume, like the ones they now use at bass tournaments to ensure the fish haven't been stuffed with foreign objects. You can't cheat at bass tournaments anymore. It's a nice camera, in other words, with its own dedicated feed online.

It's been three days now. Still no progress on the poop cam, as they're now calling it. On television, they interviewed a so-called criminology expert who suggested using, quote, *laxative support.* This idea quickly excited everyone. The production team immediately added a second poop cam, this one benefitting from a supposedly superior angle, plus a software update.

It's no longer a question of whether or not they'll use laxative support. Now everyone is wondering how the laxatives should be administered. Dart gun? Vapor spray? I've heard pervasive talk of nasogastric tubes. Apparently, it's legal to put tubes of almost any kind into someone who hasn't been accused of a crime, as long as the tubes are inserted by a medical professional. Then, a medical professional (it can be the same professional or a different one) can legally push whatever they want through the tubes and into the person.

In the end, they used the simplest method imaginable. A police officer put two hands around my brother's neck and told him to open wide. He put a pill in my brother's mouth. Then he told him to swallow. It's unclear if this police officer was also a medical professional. Nobody seems to care. They're all too excited about the dual poop cams.

All the online sportsbooks are taking bets on which poop cam will register a change first. The second camera, with its superior angle and software update, is the prohibitive favorite. But some say that the update may actually cause the camera's processor to overheat too quickly, slowing down operations and giving the first camera a slight edge.

———

I'm watching when it happens. They beat him with clubs so he'll stop moving. Whoever finds jewelry first gets a special police officer award. I guess he's finally a criminal now that the laxatives kicked in, although nobody goes to the trouble of determining exactly which law it is that he broke. They can't find any jewelry. No stolen items. The camera with the software update won.

Oven Blew Up

One day, our oven blew up. No food was inside, so we didn't miss a meal, but still it was a problem. We installed another oven. That oven blew up too. We gave up on ovens altogether and put an armoire full of knick-knacks there. The armoire blew up. Exploded might be a more accurate verb. Now we were really puzzled. We put a drying rack there. Explosion. Perhaps we shouldn't put anything else there, I said. Then Uncle Jim came over, and during his visit he must have stood right where the drying rack used to be. He exploded. This made us angry. I called the landlord. He couldn't remember who we were or which property of his we lived on. I gave him the address and he hung up right away. He never returned my subsequent calls. We may have to move, I explained to the kids. Why? they said. When I explained it all, they became upset, the news shocked them, because as usual they hadn't been paying attention. Don't worry, I said, none of us will ever explode. But they didn't believe me. If you're so sure, they said, prove it. I looked to my wife for support. Yeah, she said, prove it. She started crying. Then Uncle Jim walked in. We thought he had died.

Myrtle Beach

I spent some time in Myrtle Beach with EJ the Fire Breather (as she was known professionally), making a sad, see-through effort to keep up. I was in love with her, and she was in love with a different person, a pastor, and the pastor was married to yet another individual, a woman who seemed unbearably powerful to both of us, EJ and I, because we knew nothing about her. A few days prior, the pastor, who was loitering in the tent after one of EJ's shows, gave her a glossy beige tract of pages illustrating life and death and eternity. Later, when she pulled the tract out and fingered through it, trying to make the mechanism of salvation comprehensible for me just as the pastor had tried to do for her, I half-expected, based on the tone of her voice, to see my name printed on every page. But it wasn't.

Do you think I became a Christian? she asked me.

No, I said. Although to be honest, I was worried she had.

She kept bringing me back to her motel room, the ultimate insult because we both knew nothing would happen unless the pastor stopped by, in which case perhaps I could step into the bathroom and watch through a small opening in the door. It was the kind of thing I'd grown accustomed to: my desire at ten paces or more, through a window or a screen, oblivious to me. I wonder, do police dogs spend their entire lives desiring the drugs or fearing them?

I began to sense that EJ was afraid of the motel we'd chosen. And yet she never wanted to go anywhere else. She locked the door. Our air conditioner unit shuddered, then it sounded like a million wasps hitting a grain silo.

Hear that? she said.

The air conditioner?

No. Lower.

No, I said.

Good. Me neither.

Something's wrong with the bathroom mirror, she said later. It's like a movie playing at the wrong frame rate.

I can't sit in this room any longer, I said.

You're mumbling, she said.

I want seafood, I said.

Alright, she said without looking up from her novel. We put on our jackets and left, except EJ missed the door to her room. She actually hit her head on the door frame, hard.

I'm okay, she said.

Come here, I said, because I felt it would be my last chance to comfort her.

We walked past a budget surf shop, beach towels pulled taut in their windows, saying things like I LOVE HATERS and ASK ME ABOUT MY MONKEY. The sky was dark already, and the halogen streetlight in the parking lot shone blue like a glad disease. I had an urge to walk into its focal point and scream something profane, something to shock and amaze EJ, but specific words escaped me.

How much farther to the restaurant? EJ asked.

It's just ahead, I said.

It's what? she said. It's somebody's head?

Ahead, I said, pointing.

A head that doesn't belong to anyone.

No, I said. We're almost there.

You still want to be a writer? she said.

I shrugged.

What is literature to you? she said.

I don't know, I said. I can't remember.

For me, it's one long dream about trying to open a door.

———

The restaurant, when we arrived, turned out to be a bar with nothing but peanuts for food.

No seafood? I said.

They didn't have seafood. I sat at the bar and applied my forehead directly to the countertop.

Should we go somewhere else? said EJ. Can you hear me? Hey. How bad do you need food? Scale of 1 to 10.

I couldn't respond. I was ready for the pastor to show up, for everything to work itself out so I could finally be alone.

Here we go, she said, pushing peanuts across the countertop in the direction of my face, eat these, eat these. She ordered two whiskeys. Then she took the seat to my right and for some reason began flipping through all the photos in her wallet, photos of people I'd never heard of before.

This here—my friend Marcus—he repairs bicycles, he said. Once, he repaired the bicycle of a famous rapper.

Who?

Andre 3000? Does that sound right?

I shook my head.

Well, somebody like that, she said. Some famous guy.

I ordered another drink. Instead of getting down to my heart, the first drink had got stuck in my mouth like a local anesthetic. Maybe I had forgotten how to do it. The more I drank, the more sober I got. Except for my mouth.

Here's my cousin, Hannah. Do you remember her?

I declined to look at the picture at all. I knew she would be beautiful.

The table behind us seemed to be full of children with fake IDs. They filled the room with hormonal yelps and growls. I hated them with an astonishing and comprehensive hatred. Meanwhile, EJ had begun trying to convince the bartender of the tenets of her new Christian faith. The bartender, one of those stationary people who never seem to move their arms, legs, torso, anything corporeal at all, she was in turn trying to convince EJ, whom she recognized from the circus, to entertain us all with one of her famous juggling tricks.

EJ said, if you confess with your mouth that Jesus is Lord and believe—

I know, I know, said the bartender.

Well, do you believe? Have you confessed it?

If you give us a show, she said, I'll confess from right here behind this bar.

No, said EJ. You have to mean it.

Maybe I will.

I panicked. I knew that if EJ performed a circus trick for us inside this bar, and if the bartender followed suit by accepting Jesus as her personal savior, something horrible would happen to me.

Alright, said EJ as she stood. Give me something to juggle.

The bartender presented three unopened bottles of vodka.

Here goes, she said.

Suddenly I couldn't remember who killed Jesus.

Wait, said EJ, running her hand frantically over her denim pockets, where's my lighter?

The room went quiet.

Was it the state or the church or some combination? Pontius Pilate?

No, said EJ, shaking her head back and forth. I can't do the trick without my lighter.

Sleeplessness

I made an attempt to write a novel about sleeplessness, a doomed attempt, because I couldn't sleep. If I could have slept, I probably could have written a long, deeply integrated work of fiction about sleeplessness. I think that's how it's usually done. First, people sleep. Then they write. Sleeping ends after a period of time, which allows you to start something new, like writing. But when you can't sleep, staying awake never ends. It just keeps happening. Which makes everything else impossible.

I didn't know how to sleep anymore.

Eventually, I decided that the best way to sleep was to avoid thinking about sleep. It's like what Fleur Jaeggy says in *Sweet Days of Discipline*: It is only distractions, uncertainty, distance that bring us closer to our targets, and then it is the targets which strike us. Yes, I thought, if I can avoid thinking about sleep—and, by extension, avoid thinking about sleeplessness—the target (i.e. sleep) will strike me. What would it feel like to be struck by sleep? That part concerned me a little. Things rarely end well for the target. The impact is rarely pleasant. But I was determined never to think about sleeping again. And I would think about not-sleeping even less than that, less than never again. All this not thinking about not-sleeping would create a negative energy that would fuel me for years. It would give me the energy to not think about other things, more things than ever before. Eventually I would be thinking about nothing at all. I'd have enormous freedom in the arena of not-thinking. I could not think about all of it. The only cost would be that I'd have to live in a dungeon, as far as thinking goes. But in terms of not-thinking, I'd be absolutely free.

All that not-thinking required so much effort that I began to believe it would work, since effort leads to exhaustion and exhaustion leads to sleep. Instead, the more exhausted I became, the more I thought about sleep, which meant I slept less and less.

I had to conclude that trying not to think about sleep, no matter how successful you judge your effort to be, is ultimately the quintessential form of thinking about sleep. The only way to truly not think about sleep is to do it effortlessly. Meanwhile, the only thing I could do effortlessly, on account of my exhaustion, was think about sleep. I thought about the phrase *a good night of sleep* over and over. *A good night of sleep*. I could taste the cool, dark, fragrant words. *A very good night of sleep*. No, *a good night of sleep* was better because it betrayed less urgency—it was the kind of thing a well-rested person might think. *A good night of sleep*. I was going insane thinking about *a good night of sleep*.

Why do you keep shouting about a good night of sleep? said Tom, my roommate. It keeps me up at night. I can hear you through the wall.

Sorry, I said.

Tom liked to carry a pistol around our apartment, supposedly a ghost gun from a 3D printer. I could hear a clicking noise through the wall as he loaded it, unloaded it, cleaned it, or whatever it is you do with ghost guns at night.

Get some medicine, said Tom.

But I couldn't. They wouldn't schedule me for enough hours at work to qualify for insurance.

Nyquil and Benadryl only worked for two or three nights before my body learned to fend off their effects. I was living inside a permanent panic attack.

Tom shut the door to my room again. I could hear him muttering to himself in the living room while pacing.

I can hear your gun clicking all night, I said under my breath.

I thought, I've got to figure out a way to end my book about sleeplessness; who cares if I've barely begun it. Immediately, I thought of two possible endings. Either I would never be able to sleep, in which case the writing would simply stop at some arbitrary place, as if I had died, or else I would miraculously find I *could* sleep, which would make me feel good, which would make me feel bad, very bad, because after that I'd have nothing to write about. Because the truth was, I needed to feel bad in order to keep going. Even if feeling bad made true progress impossible.

If only I could find a loophole, I thought, as often happens in folk tales. The key becomes a bird. The frog becomes a prince. The best folk tales are nothing but loopholes. Everything else is stripped away, the ruthless moralizing which the genre exists to propagate is dissolved, revealing a serene, natural madness beneath. I wished my sleeplessness would become a toad so I could step on it.

Another possible ending was the explicit death of the narrator, that is, me. I could kill myself off in a fictional way. Maybe this would save my life somehow. Unfortunately, I knew I wasn't famous enough for this to resonate. Unless you're famous, killing yourself will always be widely perceived as pitiful, even if it's only a literary device. One way to circumvent this problem would be to write the ending, lock it away in a safe, publish a variety of other manuscripts until I did become famous, then open the vault and send the manuscript on sleeplessness to my agent, who would no doubt be amazed. When you don't have an agent, nobody is amazed by your writing. Once you have an agent, everything you write becomes a masterpiece, and everyone is amazed; even your friends, if they're writers, will pretend to be amazed by whatever you've written on account of the fact that they need you to pretend to be amazed by whatever they've written. Everyone is hanging by a thread because everyone is successful and nobody knows how to make money. In other words, nobody is successful financially, but they must pretend to be. The only way to succeed financially is to get a job teaching writing, a job writers hate because it makes writing impossible. Of course, I wasn't successful yet in even the most superficial sense—I hadn't been published. I hadn't been published because I couldn't sleep. I couldn't sleep because I couldn't stop thinking about sleep or sleeplessness or the fact that I hadn't been published.

Mentally, I was on my knees, thinking, I'm not on my knees. But you have to be on your knees to think that way, as everyone knows.

Writing about sleeplessness will not cure sleeplessness. In fact, it only seems to make it worse. Yet I continue anyway. Looking for a loophole which doesn't exist and never will (except in folktales). Looking for any possible way of ending it.

———

A few nights later, Tom invited me into his room. He claimed they'd taught him a foolproof method for falling asleep in the Green Berets.

Is that why you need a gun? I asked. Your tour of service?

Tour of service? he said. I've never heard of such a thing.

Well, I said, it's a cool gun.

It could kill people, he said. That's not cool. Plus it doesn't always work. If it ever kills someone, it'll be me. Now are you ready to learn to sleep? Come in here and lie down.

I'd never been in his room before. He didn't have a bed. On his desk, I saw the gun. It looked like an alien medical implement in the harsh light of the overhead bulb. He switched off the light and shut the door. We lay down on the carpeted floor like stargazers, shoulders nearly touching. He said it was a visualization exercise. The important thing was to imagine myself reclining in a black velvet hammock hung inside a black velvet room with a black velvet ceiling. After that, all I had to do was to repeat the phrase *don't think* over and over. Not out loud, he said. Just in your head.

They taught you this in the army? I said.

You're deviating, he said. Don't deviate and don't think.

It must have worked. When I sat up, he was gone. I turned on the light. The gun was gone. I turned the doorknob without opening the door, as if to make sure it was real. From the direction of the park, I heard an engine groan like a humongous machine from the future. When I let go of the doorknob, the latch clicked.

(911)

We rented an old house in a desolate area. No neighbors. Water ran orange from the tap. The bathroom was haunted. I was scared to plug electrical appliances into the walls. The area code was 911. I didn't care at first. Then the calls started coming in.

My infant drank a gallon of lemonade. Our dog stabbed my husband with a paring knife. I seem to have blown off my hand. Someone is hiding in the bushes, peeking through my neighbor's bathroom window.

It's not good to know what all goes on with people. You'll go insane.

Why do you keep answering? asked my neighbor, who apparently has an ordinary area code.

It's hard to explain, I said, but it seems to me that the less likely I am to receive good news, the more fervently I desire it.

Opera Singer

One day, some guy (I later found out he was an opera singer) drove his car through our house. My bedroom lamp happened to shatter in such a way that a portion of its ceramic base pierced his solar plexus, causing significant damage. I was sitting in what used to be the living room. I picked up the phone beside me to dial 911.

Hello, said the operator, what's your goddamn emergency?

I didn't like his tone. I tried to explain anyway: a car crashed into our house and the driver now seems to be in unstable condition because part of my bedroom lamp went through his chest.

Sounds awful, he said.

I was starting to get angry.

You talk to him, I said to the guy with the lamp through his chest (this is the guy I later found out was an opera singer)

Hello? he said.

After a few seconds, he hung up.

I'd rather die than speak with someone like that, he said.

It didn't take long. I tried to make him comfortable. What else can you do? That guy had a set of pipes.

Flight to Paradise

I got a job at a bookstore downtown. Sad work
for a writer. Each day it paints the clearest possible
picture of the gulch you've driven your life into.
Writing already meant less to me than ever before.
Maybe I'd read too much of my own work. It all
seemed full of predetermined outcomes. I couldn't
escape them in my writing, and I couldn't escape
them in my life. But I couldn't live that way
anymore. I had two kids under the age of two. I
barely survived the previous winter, a personal low
point which left its mark in the form of tinnitus, a
permanent buzz in my head which replaced silence
as the foundation of my sensory experience. If
you ever get tinnitus, don't visit online message
boards for people with tinnitus. Everyone there

is suicidal. Which won't be a surprise if you have tinnitus.

I stopped reading for a while, because it hurt to focus on the sound in my head, which is where reading happens. Then I got this job. When I began reading again, I found that my new medication, Lexapro, had turned me into a person who longs for plot in literature. The endless, banal intricacies of plot.

One day, while merchandising the religion section, I noticed a memoir called *Flight to Paradise* written by an airline pilot who crashed a commercial flight, nearly died, briefly entered heaven, then awoke from a coma months later to learn he was the lone survivor of the disaster. A disaster which was, by his own admission, entirely his fault. Yet over the course of the memoir, he makes no attempt to reckon with his guilt. Instead, the focus is on the vision of heaven. I was stunned (or as stunned as you can be by anything while on Lexapro). Maybe he really believed that the good news in his memoir justified the death of almost 200 people. He had discovered the ultimate reason to write. His book was a transference object designed to reverse the injustice of his survival. And he had found the simplest, most elegant way of doing it, by claiming that God himself had protected him from death in order that he might write this book proclaiming it so. In other words, his guilt was transferred to everyone who didn't believe in heaven. The crash was only necessary because of them. People like me.

When I picked up the book again days later, I realized I had skimmed past some important details. He hadn't crashed a commercial airliner— it was a cargo plane. His co-pilots were the only casualties. They crashed into a cemetery, directly striking a seven-story mausoleum dedicated to the memory of dead pilots. The ironies of fate are horrifying, I thought, surveying my surroundings. Maybe I shouldn't be working in this bookstore, beneath piles of books by dead writers.

But I had to stop thinking that way.

The man actually became an airline pilot *after* the crash.

One day, a man walked into the store without a shirt.

I just woke up from a coma, he announced.

Interesting, I said. And it was, actually, because I had just been reading the part of the memoir in which the pilot emerges from his months-long coma.

I was under for three months, he said. At least that's what they told me. I'm still pretty tired.

How did it happen? I asked.

I began reporting my dreams to the government at age 17, he explained. They seemed portentous. I thought it was my duty as a concerned citizen. Now I can't remember what the dreams consisted of, chiefly because the government put me in a coma and extracted them with a neurovacuum or whatever it is they use to steal dreams.

I nodded and returned to the memoir. Not a word on dreams to be found, which was admirable. If a writer must write about dreams, they should be made to seem as real as possible. Which was exactly what the pilot had done. It was the crux of the entire book. He had excellent writerly instincts. He knew when to withhold, when to give, and he rarely overexplained. How many people in the world have read this book? Probably less than one hundred. A small religious press out of Minneapolis published it. I looked them up. Their website explains that they are *recognized as the world leader in inspirational fiction* and *committed to taking Christian writing to the wider world.*

I thought, maybe I could send them a book about tinnitus, which was my own portentous dream of sorts, my religious vision. The sound of the afterlife. That was my main advantage over the pilot. I was still inside it. God blinds us, deafens us, gives us false dreams which we learn to love before he takes them away. He kills our friends. That's what the Bible calls healing. I closed the pilot's memoir. The man without a shirt was hitting himself in the head with a book from the history section, a volume on the war on terror.

Steady Work

I was a virtual photo booth attendant in a corporate museum gift shop. Then I was an errand boy at a sports journalism show about cage fighting. Later, I had a job which paid me to pretend I had a concussion. Medical students in oversized white jackets pretended to diagnose and treat me. They asked me to reconstruct the accident. All my responses were loosely scripted. I spoke in a slow, detached manner. According to the script, I couldn't remember how I got a concussion.

What brings you in? they all said.

My head is killing me, I said, and this was the one thing I always had to say first. My head is killing me. The more you say something, the more it becomes part of the essential calculus of your existence. Unless the opposite is true, and the more you say it, the more meaningless it becomes. Unless there's an even worse third option, which is that both could be true at once.

I'm sorry to hear that, they would say, because they knew they were being graded for empathy. Then they would say, Do you know why your head hurts?

Well, I was at work, I said, and I fell.

Where do you work? they said.

I work at a factory.

What kind of a factory? some of them said.

We make metal parts, I said to them.

Metal parts for what? said one guy one time.

For the insides of miniature toilets, I said to him, going off script, perhaps in the half-hope that a supervisor was listening to my feed and I would be fired.

Miniature toilets?

They're like toilets, but smaller, I said, illustrating with my hands.

Ah, he said. Thanks.

Why did you fall? they all said.

Well, I said (I always gave a dramatic, confused pause here), a coworker told me I hit my head.

What did you hit your head on? they said.

My coworker said I hit my head on a machine, I said, a line that still comes back to me at odd hours, when I can't sleep or when I'm idling in a drive-through line.

So you had an accident at work, and you passed out, they would say. Can you remember anything else about the accident?

No, I never could. That was just about the extent of the information I could give them, aside from basic background information: I was single, sexually active, I lived in the city, I had a roommate. I grew up Protestant but no longer practiced.

All I know is that my head is killing me, I said.

Can you count backwards from one hundred by seven? they said.

———

The candidates (that's what we called the medical students) traveled from across the country for this mandatory test in which they rotated through twelve rooms, mine and eleven others, confronting a new iteration of frailty in each one. I could hear the cameras swivel in their little glass turrets above both of our heads. Experts (doctors, presumably) watched the footage to grade each candidate's performances: pass or fail.

I took two medical leaves of absence. The first was for an actual concussion I got from walking into a closed glass door at the DMV; I tried to work through the injury, but whenever a medical student looked at me with anything like genuine concern, I wept. The second leave of absence was made necessary by a young candidate in expensive capri pants who, during the physical examination portion of our encounter, somehow sliced me open under the chin with her massive diamond engagement ring. A thin curtain of blood crept down my neck into my paper hospital gown, where it made a kind of map.

Oh god, said the medical student.

She dialed 911 on the phone, but the phones in the exam rooms weren't connected to anything but the office phones.

Hit the intercom button, I said, but she passed out in her swivel chair first. I had to do it myself.

Two months later, I returned. In the breakroom sat my coworkers, hunched over the tables, eating their cold, dead breakfasts. Jan, who pretended to have tennis elbow. Silas, who pretended to have dementia. A kid who carried sand-filled juggling balls around—I never learned his name or what he pretended to have. I heard a story about him. A candidate pushed the tip of an otoscope through his eardrum. Now he was deaf on one side and would be forever.

Is that why he never speaks? I asked Jan, whispering, because now I was thinking about it again.

No, she said. It's why he never juggles. I don't know why he doesn't speak.

My first candidate of the day shook with nerves. The embroidered name on his jacket read ROBOT. Then he shifted in his seat and it became ROBERT. Later, he was ROBOT again. Finger extended, he poked me in the face repeatedly.

Can you feel that?

Yes.

How about that?

Yes.

That?

Yes.

Right there? poking me in the chin.

Yes.

He jabbed my kneecaps.

How about that?

Uh-huh.

I'm going to whisper something in your ear. Tell me what it is, he said.

Alright.

Fentanyl.

Fentanyl.

No, he said. It was apple.

He shuffled around to my other ear.

Dramamine, he whispered.

I paused.

Could you say that again?

Barbiturates, he clarified, then he poked me on both sides of my face.

Does that feel the same as that?

Yes, I said.

Have you ever felt this way? Regarding your head?

No, I said, this is the first time.

Really?

Yes.

I'm gravely concerned, ROBOT said. Then he began, inexplicably, to cry.

Repentance Rebate

I'd been thinking of trying to write a movie for my friend the director, thinking of it for so long that we must have discussed it at some point, and then enough time must have passed for me to have forgotten our discussion, because almost as soon as we had settled into our table at the coffee shop with our drinks in hand, she asked me about it.

When will the script be ready?

The script?

The one about repentance rebate, she said.

Come again?

Repentance rebate, she said.

Right, I said.

She kept looking at me, waiting for some sign of compliance (she was already a powerful person at this point). Unfortunately, I had never heard the phrase repentance rebate, and I couldn't think of a reason for it to be associated with me. I didn't know what it meant. I didn't know why it was being used to ambush me here, in a coffee shop in Los Angeles, a place with such well-bleached surfaces I was actually afraid to breathe. In general, that's the effect Los Angeles has on everyone who stays for more than a year—we were all a little afraid to breathe. Maybe it's the inevitable result of being slumped over a steering wheel three hours each day, squinting at taillights through the smog.

Not only was my friend the director implying I had concocted this meaningless phrase, repentance rebate, at a previous juncture which I could not recall, but she now expected me to write a feature length film on the topic, a topic which had never been explored in cinema because it didn't exist, a topic which didn't exist because it could never exist, and a topic, furthermore, which actually sounded like it didn't want to exist. Asking for between ninety and one hundred sixty pages on this completely void concept, which supposedly I had at some point called repentance rebate. A page per minute of screen time—that's the rule of thumb.

But I couldn't say no, because my connections in the industry were vanishing. I had slipped, I was in danger of becoming obsolete. If I could collaborate with my friend the director, my fate might be altered. I might be able to walk into fancier coffee shops than this one (if they existed) with my chin up, ordering drinks and pastries without considering money. So it's easy to see why writing something, anything, for money was irresistible to me at this point, especially something which might create more opportunities for money in the future, more movies, maybe even book deals, book deals tied to advances, friends and admirers directly connected to the most hallowed institutions of film and literature… my mind was racing. So I pretended to know exactly what my friend the director meant, because she was my last and only lifeline to the realm of successful people, although I also knew simultaneously that it was a death sentence as long as the phrase repentance rebate was involved.

I said, Are you sure?

That's the one, she said, nodding, smiling, smiling and nodding. Repentance rebate.

Alright, I said.

You know who would be perfect for this role? she said. Emma Stone.

Jesus. You can get Emma Stone?

Maybe, she said with a shrug, and I felt bad for asking. Of course she could get Emma Stone now.

Did I say Emma Stone? she said. I meant Cate Blanchett.

Sure, I said. That makes more sense.

Emma Stone wouldn't be right at all, she said, laughing.

I nodded and actually spent a few seconds trying to think of a single reason, just one, that Emma Stone wouldn't be right for a movie called *Repentance Rebate* and Cate Blanchett would.

It's finished, right?

I'm sorry, I said to my friend the director, what did you say?

The screenplay—isn't it finished?

Well, I said, it's all a matter of perspective.

Why don't you look it over, make sure you're happy with it, and send it over after that?

———

Two weeks passed. I stumbled quietly through unmarked evenings. I kept going to work. I wanted to buy new shoes but couldn't decide on a style. I resolved to cook more but didn't. I saw disturbing images on the phones of strangers wherever I went, in public places. A video of two koalas beating each other bloody, for example, while in line at the Ralph's deli counter. The woman with the phone caught me staring.

They're not really koalas, she said.

Okay, I said.

A friend from high school passed through town. We went out for burgers and attempted to recreate a new version of the friendship we remembered. We made little remarks about the beer we drank. I went to a concert alone at a small venue where I got a little drunk and annoyed by the people in front of me who were only pretending to enjoy the music, which was too loud. And my ears rang for days afterward. Finally, I decided on a pair of shoes, but when they arrived, I noticed an obnoxious sheen on the fabric which hadn't been evident in the online photograph, so I decided to send them back. But I didn't have the energy to do it. The movies I watched were all about dealing with the trauma of adultery, movies of every genre.

I should have spent evenings trying to think about the meaning of repentance rebate. Instead, I tried not to think about it. I thought hard about not thinking about it. I couldn't stop. Basically, I was thinking about repentance rebate at all times. On the other hand, I couldn't think about it at all, because obviously it means nothing. A double turn. A refund for your refund. Voiding the void. I needed to write something so vague, it could be about anything. Vague and marketable. Not to mention highly filmable.

A full month passed. My despair became unbearable. I stopped going to work. Obviously this was my final assignment as a writer, and I wouldn't be turning anything in. I lived alone. My body probably wouldn't be found for days or weeks. Not that I cared. It was just something I thought about.

Finally, I pulled my bedsheet and duvet up under my chin and began taking the pills, testing my nerve, taking them one at a time. After pill number four, I noticed something strange. I could see myself from above, swallowing pills and breathing methodically, and I was tickled by how snugly I had tucked myself into bed, as if I'd believed this attention to domestic detail could somehow obscure my suicide.

I decided I wanted to live. But I didn't fully formulate the thought until I had already swallowed pill number five. Was five pills enough to kill? I didn't know. I hadn't done the math in advance. People will think I killed myself, I thought. Even in the midst my suicide, I wasn't sure if I'd done it on purpose or not. I wasn't sure if it met the definition of an attempt. And somehow (how?) this thought led me directly to the perfect idea for a screenplay about repentance rebate. The entire screenplay began to compose itself beneath the banner of this perfect idea. Then

I grew worried because I remembered I might be dying. I dialed 911. The operator asked me to describe the medication and dosage. I carefully read aloud from the label. That dosage is non-lethal, she said, even for children. By this point, I had completely forgotten my idea for a screenplay about repentance rebate.

Disappearances

1

My brother-in-law hired me to be his traveling assistant for one week. At an airport bar in Charlotte, before our connecting flight to Los Angeles, before the flight after that to Bora Bora where the work week would begin (his job involved contract work for hotels and resorts), our conversation faltered. Harrison, my brother-in-law, in an effort to course-correct, began to lecture aimlessly on his pet theory of the Higher Hive Mind (or maybe he called it Holistic Human Hives), a theory which suggested, I think, that throughout all of human prehistory, only a few people experienced the kind of consciousness we take for granted today. Everyone else functioned like automatons or insects, brains governed by dim electric currents and magnets, people with no sense of the infinite, no repressed horror, no self to make sense of, hardly people at all... this was obviously how the Egyptian pyramids were built, said Harrison. He said that cross-cultural contamination was what brought the era of human hives to an end. He sounded sad and a little wistful. I was already drunk because I had decided to go beer-for-beer with Harrison, a drinker of limitless capacity. I have poor impulse control in airports. I order too much food and stare helplessly at women.

How does all this strike you? said Harrison.

I don't know, I said. Could you prove it by inducing such a state of consciousness in people living today?

I have some ideas about that, some theories I'm working on, and I think they could be worth a lot of money to the right person, he said.

Like who? I said.

People who already have a lot of money, he said.

2

In Bora Bora, crabs do the work of rodents at night, patrolling the gutters with a percussive, mechanical menace. Dogs sleep inches from the road; it looks like they've been struck down by careless drivers. I almost hit some of them myself in our rented Fiat Panda because I was attempting to learn, under Harrison's tutelage, how to operate a manual transmission. I made the Panda lurch erratically around the road that circumvolves the island, like a model train powered by a sketchy generator, which was pretty close to the real situation mechanically, as Harrison kept trying to explain to me by repeating the story of the clutch and the drivetrain, the clutch and the drivetrain, a meaningless story, impossible to visualize, which I never even began to understand. While everyone else on the island only appeared to be driving recklessly (it was ultimately a sign of their mastery), I was actually doing it, because I had too much to think about all at once—the clutch, the gas, my error in taking this one-week job as Harrison's assistant—and it was embarrassing.

Only one other road existed, a radial offshoot which climbed up towards the volcanic peak in the island's center. Under ordinary circumstances, we could have paid for a guided hike to the peak. However, two weeks prior, a guide had disappeared into the steep wall of foliage with a small group of tourists. None of them had yet been found. The story surprised me because the island is so small—I could drive a complete lap around it in under fifteen minutes, stall-outs and all. Harrison resolved immediately to take this guided hike if it became available again. I preemptively refused. As a sort of compromise, one day during our lunch break I turned the Panda onto the steep road that climbs the mountain. I shouldn't say compromise. Whenever we were in the Panda, I just did whatever Harrison said, because I was afraid and he was confident. I stalled out twice. The second time, we traded places. Honestly, he was sort of a genius at operating that little car. Even when he was drunk. Soon, the paved road became a dirt path. Harrison continued, undeterred and almost elated, driving with a religious intensity up to the peak or wherever we were going. The vegetation began to thin, the clouds lifted (or had we lifted ourselves above the clouds?) and every aspect of the situation began to resemble a holy vision, a dream about ascension, time grew vague, and I couldn't help but wonder if we were dying, or if we had already died. My bad driving could have killed us at a previous juncture we could no longer remember. I began thinking of the job we'd been doing at the resort all week. It doesn't matter what the job was—it hardly merits a description. Anyone could have done it. There was no reason for us to be here. Harrison kept driving up, towards the peak, while a new kind of light suffused the car's interior, a light of measurable mass and weight. I couldn't stop thinking of a box I left in the wrong part of the hotel job site, the wrong area of the floor.

3

On our last night on the island, Harrison found the locals' bar. I knew something terrible would happen. Two days earlier, he had launched a campaign of coercion which concluded with me agreeing to participate in a jet ski tour. Now the guide from the jet ski tour was here, leaning on the bar. I think it was someone's birthday, an acquaintance of his. The jet ski guide introduced us to some of his friends, mostly women, people who worked with him at the tour company. Everyone we met bought us glass after glass of vodka and Sprite. Meanwhile—this is true—the jet-ski guide, whose name I can't remember, launched into an endless spiel, the point of which was to convince us to leave a good review for him on the tour company's website. He explained in granular detail the benevolent impact a single good review could have on his career, treating us like we were idiots. He had a name like Jet, although it couldn't have been that exactly. I would have remembered a jet-ski guide named Jet. Something similar. Later in the evening, he carefully tucked a single marijuana bud into my shirt pocket, a pointless gift which could only have caused legal trouble since I didn't have any means of dosing it. I grew worried, actually, that he was trying to frame me. But I also worried that if he saw me throw it away, he'd get mad.

I sipped my cocktail slowly, almost not at all, because at this point in life I was one hundred percent dependent on Xanax for sleep, and no hangover is worse than a combination Xanax/vodka hangover. Plus, alcohol made me anxious, which meant the more I drank, the more pills I needed to sleep. On the other hand, everything made me anxious, including not-drinking.

To my left, Harrison had established himself at the corner of the bar, buying drinks for everyone else while they bought drinks for him. We were extremely conspicuous, the only white people in the whole place. I think Harrison was trying to get laid. Much has been written on the subject of Tahitian beauties. I guess it's a quintessentially English erotic myth, a myth which ultimately served to clear a path for the colonizing forces of western venereal disease, hard alcohol, missionaries, and worst of all, real estate agents.

Now I was being paid by the real estate agents, or by a company contracted (like a venereal disease) by the real estate agents, which is the same thing. I was learning all about these things from a book I'd checked out at the Chicago Public Library and brought along: *The Fatal Impact: An Account of the Invasion of the South Pacific* by Alan Moorehead.

Now, in the back of the bar, I found an inconspicuous table and opened the book. Before I could begin, a woman took the chair across from me. She leaned across the table with a conspiratorial smile. Behind her, Harrison was still making a big show of spending every last one of his island francs. I heard him purchase bottle service: a fifth of Jack Daniel's for something like five hundred U.S. dollars.

Are you his brother? she said, pointing back to Harrison.

No, I said, but I married his sister.

What's your wife like?

She works for a non-profit whose goal is to eliminate the use of palm oil in fast-food.

That's great, she said. Stay right here, I'll be back.

I opened my book again, hoping she wouldn't return. The historian was on a roll, finding pockets between facts for riffs, speculations and wild digressions borne effortlessly forward by the lively source material. He wrote at length about the sexual agency and political power enjoyed by Tahitian women before the missionaries and real estate agents initiated their societal collapse. In most cases, before marriage, women were encouraged to sleep with whomever they pleased. Some of Captain Cook's crew members, when it was time to push off from the island, had to be separated from their new lovers by force. A few sailors succeeded in escaping. They were never heard from in England again. I looked up from my reading to see a fresh vodka-Sprite before me.

Your wife works for a non-profit. Where do you work? she said.

I didn't know what to say. I couldn't believe how beautiful she had become.

I used to write little articles for the internet, I said.

Like what?

Five Spiders Now Living in Your Basement that Can Kill. Nine Essential Components of a Good Apocalypse Bunker. Stuff like that.

You're taking them to the school of anxiety, she said.

Where do you work? I said.

I work for the same tour company he does, she said, pointing to Jet.

You help with the jet-ski tours?

We also offer hiking excursions. Or we did until two weeks ago. Did you hear about the disappearances?

Yes. Do you think they'll be found alive?

She shook her head, which I can still picture perfectly.

It's not that I wanted to sleep with her. I only wanted to have slept with her in the past. I was suddenly desperate to fill my past with content. I couldn't think of anything I'd done. She leaned across the table with her conspiratorial smile again. I really must be dead, I thought, or dreaming.

Recently, she said, my work has consisted mostly of erasing the missing hiking guide's reviews from the website. Good reviews, bad reviews—they all have to be erased. Listen: one of the reviews was from three days ago.

I don't understand, I said.

The review was posted over a week after the disappearance.

Don't tell me what it says.

But I have to, she said. It's only two words. Don't look.

May 24

At some point, I don't know why, I decided I would write a novel about May 24. Whatever happened on that day would dictate the content of the novel. I was a novelist who had never written a novel. I thought it would be easier, instead of going out in search of a novel, to let the novel come to me, like a day on the calendar. It was a day on the calendar, nothing more or less, May 24, impossible to rush or delay. Then the day arrived, May 24, and nothing happened. I should have expected it. Nothing ever happened, but I think it's fair to say that even less happened than usual on this day, the day of the novel. I was supposed to go out with several friends—they knew about the day of the novel—but they all canceled for dubious reasons. They might have been nervous about their capacity to fill a novel with subject matter. I tried to assure them that content rarely matters. It was a lie of course, because content is everything. In other words, style is everything. Because content is style. But they didn't read novels, so they couldn't tell I was lying, at least not right away (on the other hand, a novel really can be about anything as long as the writer has a sense of style… which is to say content). Then, at the last minute, they canceled. I hadn't really expected them to act naturally. In fact, that was what I'd been planning to write all about: how unnatural my friends were acting because they anticipated being novelized. A meditation on our inability to transform ourselves in our daily lives in the way that the artist transforms her subject matter. Now that my plan had failed, I realized this would have been a terrible novel, an immoral catastrophe, because the only person spared by this literary examination would have been me, the writer—if the book existed, there would be no getting around this damning conclusion. It would have been an evil book about the writer's supposedly superior means of moving through the world, transforming mundane experience into high culture, and I would have been forced to renounce it eventually.

Still, it was bad that nothing happened, because inside every novel there must be something. Even a man sitting in a chair, thinking; that's something. Therefore, it's misleading to say that nothing happened on May 24. When I thought about that—how even nothing happening is just a way of describing something happening—I became hopeful. I thought maybe I could write a novel about nothing, that is, something. Well, I thought, what's happening? What's happening right now? Unfortunately, what was happening was I was thinking about what was happening. I was applying the writing process to the writing process, and all those layers of removal created such a sense of vertigo I almost collapsed. I felt physically ill. My heart made a squelching sound in my head. This was why I needed my friends to appear, so that writing about writing wouldn't be completely unbearable. On the other hand, if they had appeared, I would have used them in the most monstrous way imaginable, like puppets.

In order to write, I needed the writing process to disappear. But without the writing process, obviously I wouldn't be a writer. For some reason, I couldn't accept this, the idea that I wasn't a writer. At the same time, I couldn't accept the writer's duty, which is to write about writing. For the writer, there's nothing else to write about. If the writer illuminates some other topic, it's only an accident. Perhaps, I thought, the good writers are those with a tendency to involve themselves in such accidents. But because it's always an accident, it's not something they should take credit for (which never stops them from doing so.) Can you cause accidents on purpose? Maybe, with experience, you could learn to cause accidents. Unfortunately, I didn't have experience. I'd never written a novel before. All I had was this date: May 24. And the events therein. Which amounted to nothing. Nothing but writing. Then a miracle happened. I died in a traffic accident.

Writing Fiction

Writing fiction is like trying to figure out who ate the salami by eating salami.

Writing fiction is like spending the last year of your life getting a tattoo.

Writing fiction is like building a snowman with anatomically correct genitalia, then feigning disgust when people ask if you plan to fuck it.

It's like experiencing real grief when your attempt to fuck the snowman makes it melt.

Writing is the artform almost anyone can master.

Fiction is a concept even babies understand.

So writing fiction should be properly understood as an effort to embrace anonymity, and confusion on this point is the reason so many writers want to die.

Writing fiction is like going pro in being potty trained.

It's like sending your kids away to orphanages and expecting them to track you down later in life to say, Dad, you're beautiful.

Writing fiction is like believing you invented foreplay.

I don't know exactly what Roberto Bolaño meant when he wrote, *The killer sleeps as the victim photographs him,* but if I had to guess, I'd say it's about writing fiction.

Writing fiction is like reading fiction, except you do all the work instead of half. Therefore, approximately half of these aphorisms should apply to reading fiction too.

It's like getting a life-saving hair transplant.

It's like planting an apple seed that produces a tombstone.

It's like visiting your tombstone for something to eat.

Lance, LeBron, Sam, and Polly

I didn't know it was going to be a party before I got there. When I arrived, that's when I discovered it: a party. I couldn't tell what the party was in honor of. It wasn't a holiday. I wanted to watch the Nuggets-Sixers game with my friend Roger, who had invited me. He said his friend who lived there had a projector we could use.

Instead, the projector showed a skiing contest, part of the Winter Olympics. A very small percentage of those present, maybe four or five people, sat entranced on the couch, watching, making shapes with their eyes whenever the contestants navigated a difficult turn. I didn't understand the attraction. It just looked to me like a telecast of people sliding helplessly down a hill, accumulating little concussions. I guess there was also history to consider, and tradition.

Basketball was different. It was theater, but more than that, it was music. Stephen Curry was Miles Davis (cool, utterly innovative), Nikola Jokic was Dave Brubeck (angular genius), LeBron James was Kamasi Washington (dramatic, cheesy, brilliant), etc, I won't belabor the point. Then there was the incomparable Lance Stephenson. Maybe you don't know who that is. He's recently been in and out of the league. There's a video shot from beneath the basket of LeBron James dribbling toward the camera when, from off-screen-left, Stephenson flies into him—I say flies because he's flapping his arms in the manner of a bird—knocking LeBron over, a clear foul. Then Stephenson collapses in a dramatic attempt to prove that LeBron had run into *him*. That was Lance Stephenson. His signature move was a sort of rhythmic gallop he used whenever he led a fast break, an inefficient and thoroughly baffling motion which proved to be surprisingly effective, maybe because defenders could never envision how it might lead to a pass or a shot or any other basketball-adjacent motion.

He's probably most famous for once distracting LeBron by blowing gently into his ear between plays, an image that perfectly encapsulates the way that heated rivalry often leads directly to the most profound kind of intimacy.

Roger wasn't in love with me or anything. We were simply friends, former college acquaintances who forged a friendship after graduation. And yet, if you've ever lived in Los Angeles, you know already how rare and precious this is: a friend, a real friend who knows how to laugh at your jokes, drink beer, and watch basketball.

Where u at? I texted Roger, *there's a party here.*

I walked through every open door and hallway in the house, looking for Roger. In one of the bedrooms, I found a middle-aged man, tattoo gun in hand, hunched over the thigh of a young girl on the bed. He was drawing a carrot so large and orange I could see it from the doorway.

You Julie? he said to me.

No.

Well, if you see Julie out there, tell her I'm almost ready. And hey, could you do me a favor? Could you grab my bottle of vodka from the freezer? I don't like to leave in the middle of a job.

In the kitchen, a group of people I had met through Roger stood in a circle beside the fridge. They were all future titans of Hollywood; producers, directors, camera ops, and so on. Rick, who worked for a major distribution company, was in the middle of a story I had heard once before. It was about the time his company and another company released movies starring golden retriever puppies nearly simultaneously. Rick's boss hired a graffiti artist to vandalize several of the most prominent billboards promoting their rival's movie. The artist added devil horns to the puppy and a remarkably obese grim reaper to the puppy's left. On some, he also gave the puppy a thought bubble which read, *I'm evil!*

It's the sort of thing that happens more than you think, Rick said. Just don't tell anyone I told you about it.

Clearly he was destined for major, debilitating Hollywood success. Everyone always liked him, even me. That was his horrible gift.

Erin said, Wasn't that movie sunk by allegations of animal abuse?

It's possible we paid for that too.

So the allegations were false?

Oh, no, I wouldn't say that. It's hard to shoot ethically with animals. They can't tell you how they feel. Frustration builds.

I found the vodka in the freezer and left without hearing my name called, which was a relief. I felt, as I always felt around these people, that if I were forced to talk, I would say something stupid. That was exactly what everyone here, everyone in this awful city, was most afraid of: hearing something stupid. Sensing their fear, I became afraid of it too. I think the fear came from the fact that the movie industry's model for success was unfalteringly stupid, and in order to forget it, everyone tried to talk fast and smart.

My angel, said the tattoo artist in the bedroom, could you pour me a couple fingers?

He nodded to an empty glass on the bedside table. I was looking at the tattoo, which wasn't a carrot at all. Now it was a man directing traffic in a reflective vest.

Shouldn't you wait until you finish the tattoo?

Don't worry, he said. It's a calming fluid.

I poured his vodka while the tattoo gun sputtered and gagged.

Julie, you're my angel.

That's not Julie, said the girl on the bed, and I almost jumped. I had forgotten she was there.

What's your name? he said.

Sam.

Your name reminds me of something. Know what it is? Never mind. I shouldn't say.

Tell me.

Sorry. I forgot, he said.

Finally, Roger replied to my text: *Walking back w beer, see you in a minute.*

I went out to the patio for air. Some people had a fire burning in the pit and a joint going around. I was amazed to hear my private thoughts from earlier being openly discussed; the group was in the middle of a conversation about stupid movies. I didn't know them, but clearly these were stragglers, people outside the industry looking in. Otherwise, they wouldn't have been talking about it. I felt I held some secret power over them. My power came from the fact that I wasn't trying to break in, but the opposite. And yet I felt a tenderness for them too because I could see their failure like it had already happened.

The *Jumanji* remake, for example, made a shit-ton of money, one guy was saying. He had shoulder-length hair above a tweed jacket.

Who could watch such a thing? said another guy.

I did, said a too-thin girl. It was like watching adults perform a Christmas pageant.

People love movies like that. But who? said the tweed jacket quietly, as if into a mirror.

There's a Russian saying, I said, If a person is dead, that's for a long time; if he's stupid, that's forever.

I've never heard that one, said the other guy, not the one with the tweed. He sounded suspicious. I couldn't get a good fix on what his face looked like.

Tatyana Tolstaya said it, I said. Although she didn't really say it. It's from a story she wrote.

If you know who said it, you shouldn't call it a saying, said the tweed jacket. That's misleading.

You're right, I said.

Especially if she didn't actually say it.

I'm sorry, I said.

What's your name?

Sam. I'm a friend of Roger's.

Oh! Roger! said the tweed jacket, What a guy.

We're supposed to be watching basketball now.

You like basketball? said the other guy, probably because I look like a girl. I didn't respond. The marijuana was getting into my thoughts. I rarely smoked, that was why. All at once, I was overcome by the fear that I would become a vegetarian for no good reason. There are good reasons to become a vegetarian, but I didn't have any of them in mind. It was just the marijuana working on me, presenting to me an image of a pig's rib which I would never, ever be able to enjoy again. I was thinking, people have ribs too, meaty ribs. I was feeling a tightness in my gut.

I said, Are you Julie?

The girl nodded.

You waiting for a tattoo?

A tattoo? She was mystified.

Never mind. I thought—

A tattoo could ruin my career.

I don't think it works like that, said tweed jacket. My friend's cousin is covered in tattoos...

But he was cut off by the sound of tires skidding in the road and, a moment later, glass shattering. It happened on the other side of the stone wall encircling the patio. We all paused, I guess because we were smoking. Then tweed guy got up to investigate, and I followed.

Oh Jesus, said tweed guy. Oh my god.

He rushed to kneel beside Roger, who was down in the crosswalk. The six pack of beer he was carrying had shattered on the opposite side of the intersection, twenty feet away.

I called for an ambulance.

What's the intersection? said the operator.

Hey, what's the intersection? I shouted.

La Jolla and Lindhurst, said tweed, South La Jolla and Lindhurst!

Halfway between the Museum of the Holocaust and LACMA! said the other guy.

Shut up! I said to him, What are you talking about?

Next the operator wanted to know if the car that hit him was still there. I wasn't sure at first. Although I didn't see the car, I had never heard it drive away either. No roaring engine, none of that.

No, I said, it's not.

When I was done talking to the operator, I tried talking to Roger. He wasn't responding verbally to the tweed guy, but I thought he might be listening.

Don't worry, Roger, I said, we'll be watching hoops soon. Hang in there. Roger blinked twice, as if trying to focus on me for a second. Then he shut his eyes again.

I've got a Lance Stephenson video to show you, Roger, I whispered. Classic Lance. It was the video I mentioned earlier, the one in which Lance caroms theatrically off LeBron. It was new. I wanted to show it to him in person. I wanted to ask him if I should buy a Lance Stephenson jersey, a question I knew would delight him to no end.

When the ambulance arrived, I swear it nearly hit Roger a second time. Once they had Roger tucked away inside, a burly paramedic asked me if I wanted to ride along. Before I could reply, he said, Hold on. You his wife or girlfriend?

No.

Sister?

I'm his friend.

Sorry. Got ahead of myself. Family only in the ambulance.

A tattoo on his forearm read I HURT TOO in gothic letters. Maybe I misread it. He was moving so fast.

Two months later, I ordered a Lance Stephenson jersey online, the navy-blue road jersey. I found a website selling them for forty dollars new, a suspiciously low price even with the twenty additional dollars for shipping. But I tried it.

Two weeks passed, and I worried I'd been fleeced. I emailed the customer service account. To my relief, someone replied right away:

> Hello friend,
>
> I am glad to inform you that the item you ordered has been shipped out via Global postal carrier shipment.
> The tracking number is LS628736202CN.
> It usually takes 7-12 days for delivery.
>
> Please let me know if you have any further questions. Thank you!
>
> Best Regards,
> Polly

After three weeks, it finally arrived from China in a flimsy disposable plastic container. Inside the container was a giant zip-lock bag. Inside the zip-lock bag was my Lance Stephenson jersey bearing the number one and the insignia of the Indiana Pacers, but it was green.

Green.

I'd go so far as to say puke green.

I wrote an email.

> Hi. I received the jersey, but it's the wrong color.
> I ordered the navy-blue men's swingman jersey,
> but I received something that is green. How can I
> get the blue one instead?
>
> Attached is a photograph of the jersey I received.
>
> Thanks,
> Sam

Three days later, I received a response.

> I am sorry to hear that.
>
> Thanks for your pic. Could you pls just keep
> it? After all, the price is low. We can give you a
> discount for your next order.
> What do you think?
>
> Best Regards,
> Polly

I responded.

Hi,

That would be fine if it weren't a hideous green jersey. Is there any blue or white Men's size small jersey you can send me? Otherwise I've completely wasted my money.

Thanks,
Sam

Polly responded.

Hi,

Yes. Maybe you could just keep it and order a new jersey. We can offer a discount, OK?

Best Regards, Polly

I responded.

Please either give me a refund or send me the correct jersey. Otherwise I'll have to talk to my credit card company to see what my options are.

Thanks, Sam

Polly responded.

Hi,

> Yes, I know that. We will figure it out. We are
> offering a discount for it. OK?
>
> Best Regards, Polly

I responded.

> No, that is not OK! I'm calling Wells Fargo as
> soon as they open tomorrow to report your
> business and have this transaction reversed
>
> Give me a refund.
>
> Thanks,
> Sam

Silence from Polly for one day, then another, then a third. I felt deranged. I checked my email constantly, at all hours of the day. It was affecting my sleep. I checked my email at stoplights. People behind me honked, I honked back, I screamed profanities. I couldn't believe what Polly was doing to me. She wasn't even a real person, in all likelihood. I wanted her to love me.

At last, her response:

> Hi,

What if you got another jersey for $45?
Our company is small and always on the brink.
Please. I hope you understand.

Best Regards,
Polly

By this point I understood their program
perfectly: reply to every one of my emails until I
went away. I wrote:

Polly,

If you knew why I ordered this jersey, you would
weep. But I'll never tell you.

Sam

I didn't think Polly would reply to that one,
but I was wrong. She wrote:

Hi,

I am sorry to hear that, but I understand.
Remember, we can still give you a discount.

Best Regards,
Polly

Letters Become Bricks

You never know when one thing might become another. Like the letters I wrote—they all became bricks before I could mail them. Little gray concrete bricks. I didn't have any use for the bricks, so they formed a pile in the corner of my living room which grew and grew with each subsequent failure of a letter. A thin layer of powdered concrete coated the floor over there, in the corner around the growing, towering pile. Because I couldn't get my letters into the mail quick enough.

I tried to dissect one of the bricks. I thought maybe my letter would be inside—maybe the letters weren't turning into bricks so much as growing concrete brick shells. I carried this brick outside onto the sidewalk, placing it carefully in the exact center of the sidewalk, width-wise. Then I went back in to fetch the sledgehammer I'd borrowed from my neighbor Kenny. It took about fifteen minutes to satisfactorily demolish the brick. No letter inside, of course. But I couldn't dismiss the possibility that the substance of the letter filled the brick in powder form, mixed into the concrete somehow.

Fortunately, a friend of mine worked as an aid in a nearby university laboratory. I brought her the crumbled remains of the brick at an appointed time. In a petri dish, she mixed some of the concrete powder with drops of a purple fluid and placed the dish beneath a microscope. She operated quickly, efficiently, and silently— priestess of the observable world in her flowing white lab coat. After a few minutes hunched over the microscope, muttering prayers, she looked at me.

Looks like these bricks are thirty years old, she said.

That was impossible. *I* was thirty years old. The now-demolished brick had appeared on my kitchen table two weeks ago, in place of a letter I hadn't finished writing.

The next week, I tried a different approach. I actually mailed one of the bricks, hoping it might become a letter again en route to its recipient. I boxed it up and paid an exorbitantly high postage fee due to the weight.

Three days later, my brother called me up.

Why did you send me a brick? he said.

Ah, damn, I said.

I have a family, you know, he said.

Right.

You can't just send me bricks.

I'm sorry, I said.

I'm mailing it back to you, he said.

The pile of bricks grew larger and larger until I decided to stop writing letters. Then I thought I might as well build something, since I had so many bricks. Besides, I had lots of free time now that I wasn't writing letters. I carried them one by one into the back yard. Technically, I shared the yard with the other occupants of our building, but nobody ever went out there but me. In nice weather, I liked to lie down in the grass and listen to the power lines hum and thrum overhead. Sometimes a helicopter flew past, or a bird.

The only structure I could think to build was a small outdoor fireplace with a chimney. I borrowed my neighbor Kenny's wheelbarrow, mixed up an old bag of concrete, and got to work pasting bricks together in the proper shape—an arched mouth and gently sloped belly leading up to a hexagonal chimney column. Unfortunately, I was one brick short—I needed one more to finish the uppermost row of the chimney. No problem, I thought. I'll go inside and try to write a letter.

Except this time, the letter didn't become a brick. Of course, I thought. Just when I need a brick, I get a letter instead. So I sealed the letter in an envelope and mailed it, hoping it might become a brick on the way. Then my brother would call me up, complain, and mail the brick back to me, and I'd have a brick.

Hello? I said when the phone rang three days later.

What is wrong with you, said my brother.

I'm sorry, I said. I noticed he was actually crying. Or maybe he had allergies—I couldn't remember if he had allergies or not.

Why would you send me this? he said. This awful letter.

Chicken Marriage Sandwich

Instead of eating, I decided to throw the chicken sandwich away, but I couldn't bring myself to touch it.

When I looked down again, the sandwich had disappeared

Don't look, I thought, but I looked in the trash can. No sandwich. I looked all over the floor. I opened the cabinets, I moved the groceries and tupperware in the cabinets all around, from side to side, in search of the missing chicken sandwich. I couldn't decide if I was still hungry, which meant I couldn't decide if I had unknowingly eaten the sandwich.

In the bathroom mirror, I examined my teeth for signs of chicken or bread or slaw or pickles.

What I found in my teeth was small and green, which might have been lettuce from lunch. Or else it was pickle from the chicken sandwich. The pickles added a nice crunch to the sandwich, I thought. Wait, I thought, how do I know that? Was it because I ate the sandwich? Or did my wife mention the pickles earlier? I looked at someone in the bathroom mirror. It was me. I was trying to decide if I should make myself throw up. I wasn't confident I could recognize a regurgitated chicken sandwich. It might look too much like my lunch. Plus, if I threw up now, it might make me hungrier later, and there was nothing to eat around here except for a chicken sandwich. If I could find it. Which I doubted. I had already spent too much time looking. The longer you look for something like a chicken sandwich, the less likely you are to find it. Perhaps it learns to self-camouflage. All I could do was dry heave. Perhaps a chicken sandwich can self-camouflage so effectively that it actually becomes something else, it transubstantiates, which is what makes it so difficult to find.

I couldn't find the sandwich, and that meant I couldn't eat the sandwich. Stop, I thought. But the idea that eating the sandwich would save my marriage had already entered my head. Now I was more than willing to eat the sandwich because of this mistaken notion. If only I could find it. I swore to myself I would eat the sandwich if I found it. My mind was swimming with such ideas about the sandwich. My marriage sandwich. I knew it wasn't a marriage sandwich, but I didn't care. There is no such thing as a marriage sandwich, a sandwich which must be consumed in order to save your marriage.

Two Bathtubs in Memphis

Duckworth's used to be a brothel, and before that, a hotel. Now it's a bar. No liquor or taps, just bottles of beer and one food item, the Soul Burger (highly recommended.) Upstairs, above the main bar, you can walk through a labyrinth of old empty hotel rooms. On crowded nights, they sell bottles of beer from an additional makeshift bar up there. One of the upstairs bathrooms contains a bathtub in which Ray Charles once allegedly reclined to get high. But there are two bathrooms, and they both have old metal bathtubs, and nobody seems to know which bathtub ought to be venerated as the one Ray Charles shot up in. As a result, the power of the story is totally negated. As soon as you encounter the problem of the second tub, it's easier to imagine it didn't happen at all.

I used to be the drummer in a country band that booked regular gigs here. That's how I eventually got to know Robyn, the bartender. She didn't know which bathtub it was either.

How do you think he got into the tub, I said, whichever one it was?

What do you mean?

Wasn't he blind?

Ray Charles?

I nodded.

He was blind. Not crippled.

Did you know, I said, that his brother drowned in a laundry tub as a child? Maybe he was thinking of his brother while he was high. I like to imagine it so.

Ever done heroin?

I shook my head no. The guy next to me, a guy I'd never seen before, chimed in. He said, my sister was maimed in a hit and run, but I don't think about her prosthetic limbs every time I see a Hyundai Sonata.

I wanted to ask him what he thought about instead, but I couldn't, my disdain for him was so immense.

It's the tub in the first bathroom, by the way, he said.

Which one's the first one? I said, because there were two staircases—the bathroom you encountered first depended on which staircase you chose.

How should I know? he said. I never go up there. I just heard it was the first one. Whichever one you encounter first.

As for me, I went upstairs a little too much, probably. I had met all three of the women I'd ever really loved up there, including my ex-wife. Somehow this was known to Robyn, the bartender, and she thought it was funny. Number four is here tonight! she would say whenever I stopped in. Or else she would make a show of using her phone and say, sorry, just texting Daphne. Got some urgent chores for her to tend to upstairs. I'd already met Daphne somewhere else, so it didn't fit the pattern. But Robyn didn't care. Daphne was a mutual friend of ours and also a musician, the leader of a different, better country band. Was I enamored with her the way Robyn and all my friends suspected? Not exactly. But her music was certainly hard to forget.

On this particular night, Daphne actually appeared, actually sat down beside me. I think she had already been drinking. But it was late, and so had I. Actually, we were approaching the time of night when I usually ordered a Soul Burger.

And I had. Robert, the cook, pushed it around the griddle. His only job, to make Soul Burgers. On busy nights, he had one or two going at all times. Just before Daphne appeared, one of the knobs on the griddle caught fire. Nobody seemed to care or even notice. Ten minutes later, the flame extinguished itself.

I saw Kristen here last night, said Daphne.

People keep telling me that, I said.

Kristen was my ex-wife, and I hadn't seen her in years. We'd met upstairs in the room with the red lightbulb. The band downstairs played an Elvis song, and I asked if she'd ever been to Graceland. Now, sitting beside Daphne, who suddenly seemed to look quite a lot like Kristen, I inspected my reflection in the mirror behind the bar. I looked exactly like myself, like a picture of me, which was upsetting.

I was upstairs, just catching my breath alone when she appeared, said Daphne.

Other people had told me this story before, and I decided at some point not to believe it was her. In my view, it wasn't her ghost up there but a dream we shared, a communal delusion. Because we couldn't find any evidence of her death. We just began seeing what may have been her ghost. It had been a difficult year for everyone. Isn't that when communal hallucinations generally take hold? For months, people had mentioned seeing Kristen upstairs. Usually, I was beyond discussing it. What was different about this particular night? I couldn't keep my hands in any one place—they kept moving around. Meanwhile, the jazz band across the room was locked into such an obscure, quiet groove, they must have forgotten they were playing in public.

The longer I sat on my barstool, looking at the picture of myself in the mirror, the more Daphne seemed to look like Kristen. I guess I was slowly forgetting what Kristen looked like, unlearning her face, her gaze, her voice, and it seemed that Daphne helped me reverse this process, but maybe it was an illusion, maybe Daphne's face was simply replacing Kristen's, taking up residence in the Kristen part of my brain, and I didn't know why. Daphne took me by the crook of my elbow.

Upstairs, we sat in the room with the red light bulb, drank our beers, and made small talk about our respective bands. I went on and on about how much better hers was than mine. She didn't want to pursue the subject for obvious reasons, but now I was lost, I couldn't stop talking about it. I got worked up about the last show of hers I had seen. I don't know why. I began to cry. I guess I just wanted her to know about her music, the effect it had on me.

Hold on, she said, I'll get another round, and she went downstairs with our empty bottles in hand.

After an interlude of two or three minutes, either Daphne or Kristen appeared and handed me a beer. I looked at her again. I started to say something, then stopped. I wanted to choose my words carefully. I was afraid that if I said the wrong thing, one of us would vanish. It was a happy sort of anxiety—I wasn't afraid of her judgment, but of upsetting something bigger, a larger design which probably isn't real.

Are you happy? I said, finally.

She laughed.

You know, you ruined both my other relationships, I said. Not just the one before, but the one after too.

She thought that was funny too.

What's it like? To be past all this wanting?

It's like the only job you ever had was acting in the same play, she said. Not an important role—a bit part. Still, you cared about it. Then one day, for no reason, the theater disappears.

Hey, I said, do you know which bathtub is the one?

Yeah. Would you like me to show you?

I would.

She walked past one bathroom door and opened the other. When she turned the light on, the bulb overhead made a sputtering noise like a large insect choking on prey.

See this little patch of rust? she said, pointing. That's how you know it was the tub he used.

The rusty spot looked like a tenor saxophone.

How did it get there? The spot? I said.

I think a man was murdered here. His blood corroded it.

Was it him? I said, my voice catching, although I knew no such thing happened to Ray Charles. He died in a Beverly Hills mansion, surrounded by family and friends.

No, she said.

Lie down with me, I said, I'm cold.

I can't do that, she said. You're thinking of someone else.

Outside, snow fell. Rarely do I get the chance to drive home through snow. I should have stopped for gas, but there's only one gas station between the bar and my house; on the approach, I noticed a large stray dog posing beneath the sodium-vapor lamps, not an uncommon sight in Memphis. I drove past. In my rear-view mirror, the car behind me pulled in.

Sometimes, you witness something that doesn't become useful until later; you have to become a different person first. You may need time to reconfigure the thing that happened into the thing you want or, if you're lucky, the thing you need. With that in mind, I think it's worth noting that this story I'm telling you now happened long ago. Our marriage, mine and Kristen's, ended even longer ago than that. And our first meeting, in that same red room where I learned her name? You see what I'm driving at here. And yet one day I was at home, drinking coffee alone, when I remembered this whole story about our last encounter, just as I'm telling it to you now. If you had asked me about it before then, before the day of my re-remembering, it might have been a different story entirely. It might have been about how I once ordered a Soul Burger I forgot to eat.

My Idea for a Building
Plus
One Joke

I had an idea for a building. It was simple. It had to be; I didn't have much space in my apartment. I kept my idea for a building in the top of my apartment's rear stairwell, which meant my idea for a building was a genuine fire hazard. In the event of a fire in the front stairwell, I would be forced to smash through my idea for a building with a hammer. Whether or not it was even possible to do so in under an hour was debatable. But I decided to live with the risk. There was no other place to put it.

I'm embarrassed to say what my idea for a building was.

My idea for a building was a concrete cube in every way but one, which was this: the idea for a building featured a slot I could open, which led to a crawl space with just enough room for my body to fit inside. Entering was difficult. I pulled myself in with an idea for a rope. Once inside, I pressed an idea for a button, and the slot closed, concealing my presence in the idea for a building from the outside. Inside, the air was cool. I had some ideas for a surreptitious ventilation system which kept the air cool and fresh. And the darkness was absolute. It wasn't an idea for darkness, but darkness itself. When I was ready to exit, I would press the idea for a button again, wait for the slot to open, then wriggle out slowly (the idea for a rope was useless on the way out).

One afternoon, while I was inside the idea for a building, the idea for a button stopped working, which meant the slot wouldn't open. I was trapped.

I began to pray. I said, God, if my idea for a building is what's going to kill me, please make it swift. I can't stand to suffer for long inside something that's brought me such happiness.

I said, God, maybe you're right. My idea of happiness needs to be reshaped entirely.

I said, God, help, help, help.

Finally, God, in His great mercy, answered my plea. He gave me an idea for a new button, an idea which came out of nowhere. I pressed this new idea for a button. The slot opened. I wriggled my way out.

Have I told you the one about the surgeon?

Somewhere, in some far-off idea for a building, a surgeon walks into an idea for a surgery room.

Hello? he says. Is anyone here? Where is everyone? Hello?

By this point his heart is full of dread.

Van Gogh at Work

They made a movie about Vincent Van Gogh, animated by a team of painters in the style of Van Gogh's paintings. It's called *Loving Vincent*. The tagline is *the world's first fully painted feature film*. Sounded like a gimmick to me, but my father-in-law played it the day after Christmas, when we were all sitting in his living room, recovering from a disastrous *Jeopardy!* viewing experience, by which I mean that my brother-in-law had named a pornographic actress in an attempt to complete a clue regarding a Steven Soderbergh movie. He was thinking of the wrong Soderbergh movie, but my wife's uncle said, Who? and appeared to google her name on his phone. A taut silence filled the room. My wife's uncle spent some years going to recovery meetings and therapy for what he now openly referred to as his *internet sex addiction*.

As a result, we were all in a strange mood when the Van Gogh movie came on, feeling slightly displaced and out-of-sync with the passage of time. However, it proved to be savvy programming on my father-in-law's part. Something about the old-fashioned artificiality of the movie's renderings calmed us. I suppose I can only speak for myself—maybe everyone else went on feeling vaguely panicked while the movie played, while I got lost in the dancing, sour yellows and whirling blues of the imitation Van Goghs.

The main question the movie asks is, did Van Gogh really shoot himself in the abdomen, out in the countryside by one of his canvases? It's a detective movie. The man from the famous portrait with the yellow jacket plays the detective. In the process of trying to deliver a letter to Vincent's brother (already deceased, it turns out), he becomes fixated on discrepancies in local accounts of Vincent's death. Was it murder or suicide? Or some strange combination of the two? Suddenly, it occurred to me that this may have become an urgent question for the people who made the movie, the hired painters. Perhaps they felt that by spending countless hours imitating Van Gogh, they were doing more than loving him, as the title suggests, but actually becoming him. And when you're in the process of becoming someone, it's important to know if that person killed himself in the midst of making the very same work you're attempting to duplicate.

Now the movie felt less relaxing. The oil paint washed across the screen in grotesque tides of color. When I saw red, I thought of blood, the blood of the animators, who must have reached a breaking point. The fatal gunshot is never actually animated. A tasteful omission, and necessary for the purpose of giving viewers space to draw their own conclusions. Still, I couldn't help but imagine that although it was in the script, they couldn't keep the animators assigned to paint it alive. They dropped dead by the dozen, I thought, infected by Van Gogh. Killed by the feeling that they were simultaneously making the best and worst paintings of their lives.

I squeezed my wife's hand. She was asleep. Everyone was dead asleep but me. I married into a family of easy sleepers. My family is the opposite. Nobody knows how to sleep. My mom watches television all night because she can't sleep, and my dad has sleep apnea. His sleep apnea is a symptom of asbestosis, the result of inhaling too many asbestos fibers while making non-essential facility repairs at a nuclear power station in Oconee, South

Carolina, a short drive from our house. At the time he was hired, everyone already understood the danger of asbestos exposure, his supervisors included. They needed the work done anyway.

Cheap Therapist Says You're Insane

I'm on the phone with my therapist when I hear a commotion in the kitchen and, looking up, discover my roommate, possessed by a demon. He has returned early from work. I'm at the opposite end of the apartment, near the living room window, the only place in the apartment where my phone works. Service is bad, I suspect, because the walls are lined with lead paint. Sometimes, even beside the window, I have trouble making out what my therapist says—a potentially hazardous situation for me. Suppose I tell him a story about my week. A story about how I didn't sleep for three days and on the third day, a pizza crust I was gnawing on clamped down on my cheek with all the ferocity of a cornered animal, biting me back. My life has been in a tailspin ever since, I conclude, and I don't recognize my own thoughts.

Suppose I tell my therapist this story, and in response I hear him say, Sounds like you're dying. Death. Now, what he actually said was, Sounds like you're trying your best. But it's too late. The misinformation is a part of me, changing me in nameless ways, at a molecular level, with no going back. Something like that has almost certainly happened. Probably more than once. How should I know? Unfortunately, it's a risk I have to take because there is nowhere else for me to make the calls. I can't very well sit down in a coffee shop and start making strange utterances about my mother, or pizza. The private rooms in the library are always occupied. The apartment has to do, bad service and all. I can't complain too much because his hourly rate is extremely affordable. Except now my roommate has come home from work early, possessed by a demon.

Hold on, I tell my therapist.

I'm talking to my therapist, I say to my possessed roommate. Can I have the apartment for another twenty minutes?

Oh, sure. I'm sorry. Take as much time as you need, says my roommate, possessed.

Thanks, I say.

No problem. I totally forgot about your appointment on Wednesday nights.

That's okay.

He leaves.

I'm back, I say to my therapist, and I think my roommate is demonically possessed.

What makes you think that?

I say, Well…

What does he sound like?

He just sounds like himself.

So he seems pretty much like a normal guy. And that concerns you.

What are you suggesting? I ask.

I hear him mumbling through the distortion.

Could you repeat that? I ask.

He says, You're in Spain.

No, I'm not, I say. I've never been.

Yes, you are, he says.

That's not why the signal's bad, I say. I'm in Chicago. I think it's the lead paint in the walls acting as a Faraday cage.

RIP Bobby

I had a friend, an aspiring novelist living in Culver City whose next project, so he said, was to drive his car directly into a wall and write about it.

Can't you just make it up? I said.

No, he said. I must make contact at forty miles per hour, minimum.

When pressed for more information, he said that another writer had undertaken a similar project, identical basically, but the book he produced was condescending, small-minded, pedantic, and overly essayistic. This revolting book was immediately hailed as a triumph in all the most important literary magazines and newspapers. It was probably the worst book that would ever be written about driving a car straight into a wall at forty miles per hour for the purpose of writing about it. But it was also the first.

He's a fraud, said my friend the novelist. He probably never drove a car into a wall at any speed. I'll show everyone.

Show them what? I said.

What it means to hit a wall with your car.

This piece is dedicated to his memory. He was a promising novelist, although it's true that at the time of his death, he'd never written a word of fiction. *40 MPH* would have been his first book.

Man Against Mansion

The man spent years trying to destroy his mansion. First, he broke the bathroom mirror. Breaking the mirror broke his hand.

When his hand healed, he took a sledgehammer to the spiral stairs.

I just want a few friends, he said. I just want a small house and a simple life.

The mansion was large and difficult to destroy.

I just want to read a good book, he said, dragging the sledgehammer into the library.

Armchair

I had some friends I didn't like. I didn't like saying their names. For example, Arnold Bunk. How often in one lifetime can you safely say a name like that?

The problem with friends you don't like is that gradually, over time, you forget why you don't like them because they're your friends, and anyway you've got nobody else to rely on when your smoke alarm goes off in the middle of the night for no reason you can see.

I'm getting ahead of myself. As the story goes, my smoke alarm went off in the middle of the night. But I couldn't find it. I didn't know where all the deductive equipment could be found.

Anyway, the noise punched a hole in my head where a hole shouldn't be, and I didn't think I could go on living. Not with the hole in my head. Two holes actually. Ears! This is the story of how I got ears.

Instead of ending it right away, I went over to Arnold Bunk's house, because I hated his name so much it was the only one I could remember in a time of crisis.

They're called ears, he told me.

Fuck, I said. I think I was wailing.

This one's just about Arnold Bunk, by the way.

He had a house with a basement.

Follow me, he said, leading me slowly down the basement stairs. This was where he kept his prize possession, a machine which reads your head. In the end, you get a word. This is the word, the machine would say, that most closely corresponds to your head. Or, if you believed in the power of the machine to the same high degree as Arnold Bunk, you could say that the machine's word *was* your head. And your head was the word. Or was it that the machine was your head? Now I can't recall. Arnold carefully strapped me in. He pressed the button. The machine had only one button because it did only one thing: read your head. Unless it also became your head. The button told the machine to do it, whatever it was, the reading, and my word was ARMCHAIR.

That can't be correct, I said.

Arnold just looked at me.

Don't do that, I said.

What? he said.

Don't look at me like that. Like my head's an armchair.

I'm not, he said.

Next he placed me in front of his TV.

What could be worse than an armchair with ears? I heard everything that happened.

Missing Person

In Greenville, South Carolina, I had a roommate who once, years earlier, had gone missing. He was an assistant for a powerful D.C. lobbyist at the time. I heard about it from his brother, a high school buddy of mine. Nobody knew why he had disappeared. A week passed, then he showed up again. He quit his job and moved to Greenville around the same time I needed a new roommate.

Whenever he closed his bedroom door at night, something happened to the air in our apartment. I knew, although I don't know how, that he was doing things in that room that I should avoid thinking about.

Eventually, I developed a problem with pills which I suspect was directly related to the situation with my roommate, the air in our apartment at night, air I was afraid to breathe. Why, I asked myself, was I afraid to breathe it? My conclusion, which didn't make sense, was that the air was looking at me. I bought pills in translucent blue bottles from my coworker, Javier. I started going to church, which is maybe the strangest thing of all. The church was a ten-minute walk from our apartment. I guess I hoped that the church knew something about why people disappear and what that has to do with the feeling, the conviction, that the air looks at you.

Some of the church-goers were probably afraid of me—I was pretty thin and I wasn't sleeping much—but some of them were nice. The pastor made a point of speaking to me each week. He was one of those learned evangelical pastors who read widely, but in a closed-off way. Maybe we all do. At the time, I was working in the kitchen of a fried chicken place. The chicken batter smell permeated my clothes, my bedroom, my hair; I must have smelled like chicken to the pastor. Maybe that's how he thought of me, as the chicken guy.

At home, my roommate began closing his door earlier and earlier each night. He stopped eating dinner, I think, unless he was sneaking it into his room. I began to worry I was caught up in a phenomenon exploring the limits of its power, like a rip-tide, something difficult to control. I was on the verge of losing my job because I couldn't sleep and I couldn't wake up. I even stopped going to church. I'll just move out, I thought. I'm not strong enough for this. The books he read, I noticed, were all philosophical treatments on the possibility (the extreme likelihood, the authors might say) that we live inside a computer-generated simulation.

One night, while I was eating a turkey sandwich on the couch, my roommate sat beside me.

Something's wrong with me, he said.

Why?

I can't do that thing with my fingers, he said, and then he tried to show me what he meant.

The itsy-bitsy spider?

You try, he said.

To my horror, I found I couldn't do it either. My left index finger couldn't find my right thumb and vice versa.

I lost my job. Maybe I had given up. The air in our apartment was looking at me, watching. I had to move back in with my parents across town.

Before the move, I walked to church one last time. I felt someone behind me on the sidewalk. I decided not to look. It's probably nobody, I thought, or else it's somebody minding their own business, walking to the hardware store to buy body bags. No, not body bags, I thought, trash bags. I tried to generate good thoughts for myself. I thought about what kind of job I might get next. I thought about buying a car.

At church, I sat in my usual pew, near the back. A minute later, my roommate opened the sanctuary doors. I knew he would sit beside me and pretend to be a stranger. But he didn't. Instead, he walked past my pew and continued in the direction of the pulpit, the stage, the empty risers for the choir. The organist played a brisk, spiraling melody while people stood, mingling cautiously, waiting for their cue to sit, the key change. At the front of the sanctuary, my roommate touched the pastor. He put his hand on the pastor's shoulder like an old friend, drew him in close, spoke into his ear. Everything else grew quiet. I thought I heard him say, I'll wake up at any moment. I looked down the length of my pew. It was empty. The organist changed keys, but I couldn't sit. Nobody could. We all watched my roommate bring his hands together, like a child learning to pray.

Shivering in Virginia

On a Saturday night somewhere in Virginia, in the middle of the game against the fourth-ranked Orange Team University, Maroon Team University's quarterback, no. 8, begins visibly shivering—afterwards, some will say it was a seizure, others will say a panic attack, and still others will take the medical staff's official post-game explanation at face value: he was cold—and on the next play, from shotgun formation, he misses the snap. The snap isn't bad. He just misses it, probably due to his shivering plus whatever else is happening to his psyche. The ball grazes his left shoulder pad. A horror is unfolding, a horror which has nothing to do with football, by the way, and the football flutters awkwardly to the turf while no. 8 shivers and lets the horror unfold. The football field is like a cemetery and he really is cold. The ball is loose, but he can't remember how to behave or what the ball signifies when it's on the ground, on the grass of the cemetery, and this is what disturbs us, the viewers, most. We will never be certain what we do is right. No. 8 can't remember what to do, he can't remember why he's shivering, and worst of all, he can't recall a single detail of his life up to this point, which concerns him, because it means he could be anyone. And anyone else could be him. After the play (fumble recovered by Orange at the Red 25), it takes a heroic mental effort for him to walk off the field, onto the sideline with his teammates. He shivers. Nobody touches him. On the field, all the tombstones are lining up. Not a single person joins him on the sideline; nobody wants to talk. No medical staff, no coaching staff, no teammates. He shivers and sinks into his shoes.

Thirty minutes later, one of the student trainers walks with no. 8 through the tunnel, into the locker room, where for some reason the lights are off. They can't find the light switch. The trainer stumbles around in the dark, muttering, looking for the light switch. He curses and uses his phone's flashlight to scan the walls. No. 8 has two thoughts at once. I'm dying. No I'm not. Did someone move the fucking light switch? says the trainer. It used to be right here.

Let's watch the play again. Before the snap, the slot receiver and the wideout eye one another for an extended period of time. Then, at the moment the ball is snapped, they make the exact same move off the line, an ineffectual double jab step and spin which can't be anything close to what the coaches drew up. Don't we all live in the same world? And aren't we all becoming more like one another with each passing day (although we must pretend to embody the opposite effect)? In summary, something mysterious happens to the slot receiver and the wideout, they accidentally mirror one another, and meanwhile no. 8, the quarterback, is lost and seeing tombstones. He needs somebody to mirror. That may be the root of the problem. The game is a lingering formality at this point. Orange is up 21 with eight minutes left. Angry fans begin to leave. Days later, when no. 8 announces his retirement from football, many of the same fans are overwhelmed by a sense of cosmic well-being which is difficult to explain.

No. 8 transfers to a smaller school. He keeps waiting to die in his sleep but for obvious reasons (he's young, healthy) this never happens. He studies computer science. His name is Marcus. Now he knows how to write code.

3:30

Walking the city grid at 3:30 pm with all the other unemployed people. We pretend not to notice each other. It's a deal we struck up when we got tired of explaining. Although I'm sure we all have our reasons. My tennis elbow, for example (which, I'll have you know, has made the composition of this document nearly unbearable).

Out of nowhere, a cat tears eagerly across the sidewalk and into the street, like a good student answering a difficult question, where it dies beneath the wheel of a Cadillac old enough to be suffering from several diagnosable psychological disorders.

My grandmother believed we all have the psychic capacity to receive premonitions. But we avoid them because they're mostly unbearable. We avoid them with such vigor, we don't know we're avoiding them. We don't know what the *them* refers to.

Nobody knows what to do about the cat, so we default to our standard position. We pretend not to notice. We pretend it's not real. Strangely, it's not a new experience for me because I've read several Kobo Abe novels, and he litters the books with descriptions of dead feral cats, though it never has anything to do with the story. Still, I've noticed.

This is why I've failed so far in my career to write essays. I never provide the appropriate details. Instead, I'll mention Abe's dead cats or else float the idea that *The Woman in the Dunes* is an allegory for concussion without providing evidence. Then my editor will ask, do YOU have a concussion? And I'll be forced to respond, Yes. How did you know?

No more essays for a while.

At Walgreens, it occurs to me that if some ne'er-do-well decides to spread toxic salve on the crested tops of the deodorants, nobody will know until the coroner reports get filed and possibly not even then. I ask to speak with the manager.

I'm the manager, says some kid.

What I'm proposing, I say to the kid, is a new job. The job is to inspect the deodorants regularly in order to prevent tainted product from reaching the public. If all goes well, we could expand eventually to shampoos and conditioners and even various foodstuffs. I could begin this job tomorrow. For the sake of transparency, I should add that I suffer from tennis elbow and a recent concussion, but I doubt these conditions will affect my job performance.

Get lost, says the kid. He can't be any older than twelve.

I look at him with a look that says, you just blew a fucking million-dollar idea. It's a look I learned from television, where it appears with a surprising and almost sinister regularity.

A few minutes later, I return with sugar in my pockets and begin sprinkling it on some of the hair care products, just to scare them a little. But before I make it to the deodorant/shampoo aisle: an ambush. I should have sensed it coming. I should have been listening. They toss me out into the street.

I need some deodorant, I scream.

Sadly, it's true. I ran out of deodorant this morning.

Fortunately, everyone outside pretends not to notice.

Realistic Outcomes

They say Einstein never learned to tie his shoes, he said.

Seems unlikely.

You're right, he said. I shouldn't have said it.

It's not impossible, I said. Just unlikely.

How could he have traveled at all, with those shoelaces flopping around? How could he have gone to college? He would have kept on stepping on his laces, tripping, falling, hitting his head.

Maybe he wore shoes without laces: loafers.

I'm sorry, said my friend. I'm sorry that I implied Einstein kept hitting his head.

It's ok, I said, hey, don't cry.

I'm sorry I implied that instead of going to college, he suffered an extended series of traumatic head injuries. Oh god.

I don't think you did.

And it follows directly that the Nazis would have perfected an atomic bomb first. Because Einstein wouldn't have played a part, not even a small role, in American development of atomic weapons. Because of his interminable string of concussions. His shoelaces swinging malevolently beneath every alternating step like some primitive critter trap.

Even so, I don't think that's a realistic outcome, I said. Even if Einstein didn't exist. He had almost nothing to do with development of the bomb.

Who cares, he said. Poor Einstein.

Wait, I said, what are you doing?

But he was gone, having leapt from the bridge we were traversing by foot, the Arthur Ravenel Jr. Bridge in South Carolina which spans the Cooper River between Charleston and Mount Pleasant, on May 24, 2011.

My Shoes

I almost missed my appointment with the ophthalmologist because I noticed something about my shoes. The shoes scared me. The shoes seemed not to be mine. I couldn't remember buying them. I couldn't remember wearing them. I couldn't force myself to put them on. They were nondescript dark green (or maybe faded black) canvas shoes. I felt strongly that the shoes had been done to me, like the man who passed out and woke to find stitches in his side, a vague ache in his bowels.

What happened, he said.

We took your kidney, said some well-gloved people, and now that it's gone, you'll feel better.

Why did you take it? said the man, and where has it gone?

But they asked him to be quiet, for the sake of his recovery, which they were quite optimistic about.

Flo-Rite

My dad kept a two-gallon pesticide sprayer in the basement. FLO-RITE, it said in raised letters across the handle. In summer, he used to walk through the backyard, gently tapping the earth in intervals with the long, slender nozzle, dispensing chemicals. Afterwards, he walked into the house and continued to spray, lining the baseboards with poison, wetting the carpet against the wall. Every year. Was it pesticide or insecticide? Now I'm not certain. It could have even been herbicide. Whatever it was, he believed it would keep the spiders away from our beds.

Spiders? I said. What kind?

Slippery little black ones, he said.

I was relieved. I had been picturing something bigger and hairier.

What's wrong with slippery little black spiders? Do they bite?

No, he said, shaking his head solemnly, but when they gang up on you, it can be bad.

I'd like to see that.

I don't think you would. You're too young for that kind of reckoning.

His voice was pitched up a notch, like someone I'd never met. The chemical fumes must have been toying with certain important parts of his brain.

Why do we kill them if they don't bite? I said.

But the conversation was over, he was putting the FLO-RITE away and whistling.

Later, at dinner, my mom produced a lump of pork from the oven. It was a pig when it had gone into the oven. When it came out it was pig-shaped pork. The oven had accomplished this. Our house was full of such awesome tools. The shower, for example. The bed. The central air and heat. All meant to speed along or induce change which would have occurred eventually in nature, but it might have taken months. Or longer. The pig would have died eventually and cooked in the sun. What would its death have meant then?

My mom called for my older brother to come to the table, but he remained in the living room, playing Xbox at a terrifically high volume, one of those games in which you shoot an antique rifle into the soot-covered landscape of a foreign country. Our kitchen reverberated with gunfire and the mortal grunts of my brother's enemies.

Wait a second, said my dad, did you cook this in the oven? I sprayed in the oven.

No you didn't, said my mom.

I did. I sprayed it up and down.

We all three stared at our plates of pork.

I've seen spiders in there, he explained, his head laid sideways across the kitchen table, beside his plate. In the living room, my brother activated a series of explosions, bombs, a sound which pulled me away from the table, into the living room, because I was afraid to look at my dad's head on the table any longer. I was afraid he might say something it would take decades to forget, or else he would cry.

On the screen, I couldn't find any trace of war at all. My brother's character, a sleepy-looking soldier, stood motionless on a beach, staring across an ocean. It wasn't a bomb I'd heard. The sound came again when a wave crashed.

The Story Behind the Stories

You may be wondering which of the previous stories, if any, contain details drawn from my life. Let's ignore the fact that I spent more time on these stories during the past year than I spent attending to my life—in other words, these stories were my life, which is sad, considering how slim this book is. But if we stick to widely accepted interpretations of words like "fact" and "fiction," which I'm more than happy to do, it should be easy for me to point out, for your enjoyment, the places in this book where the two overlap.

I was born in Anderson, South Carolina, a suburb of a suburb which calls itself the Electric City because, I don't know, they must have spent a lot of money installing power lines in the early twentieth century (I shouldn't have to do research for this story, since it's all about me.) I don't recall much about my first years. I'm told I liked to push toys across the floor, and I was afraid of dogs, no matter how friendly or small. I grew. I learned to talk. What else? In the aftermath of a shipwreck, I was separated from my parents at sea. I fell into the wrong lifeboat. The chaotic waves, winds, and currents of the storm quickly ushered my lifeboat in the opposite direction of all the others. A pirate ship rescued us. One of the pirates taught me to read and write. His name was Dingy. When his ship docked and it was time for us to part ways, he gave me his copy of *Jesus' Son*, which was the book he'd used to teach me to read. Remember, he said, if you want to write like Denis Johnson, you have to live like he did, at least a little. We shed tears and parted ways. I developed an opioid problem while hitchhiking across the country, making corrosive friends and writing little. After ten years of that, I got sober. I became a Christian. I began to lead what I thought was the life of a writer, a more disciplined life. I got a twitter account. I made a few enemies and no friends. My enemies hated me because I refused to submit to an up-and-coming literary magazine called *Suck My Toes Quarterly*. They called me "an enemy of the literature of the real" and "Little, Brown-noser and Co." As their numbers grew and their defamatory attacks became more vicious, I logged off forever. I needed money.

Fortunately, my uncle died around this time. As his only known direct relative, I inherited his estate. I liquidated his estate immediately and moved to Brooklyn. To my surprise, this was where all my twitter enemies lived, except they were placing pieces in *The Paris Review* now instead of *Suck My Toes Quarterly*, because the editor of *SMTQ* was now the editor of *The Paris Review*, a shift in the literary landscape which my enemies had foreseen long ago thanks to countless nights spent studying twitter. I had to flee New York. As I prepared to leave, all my enemies begged me to stay—they swore they were my friends now because they'd discovered I was rich. Too late, I said. They spat in my face as I walked out the figurative door. Forlorn, I enlisted in the army. But even the army rejected me because I'd been published in the wrong indie lit magazines. Great, I thought, maybe now I can start writing like Denis Johnson, because he had dodged the draft in his youth, and now I've had a similar experience, even if it was the reverse in some ways, since the army had dodged me. But I still wasn't writing like Denis Johnson. Somehow, I got into the Iowa Writers' Workshop.

Jackpot. Months later, the former editor of *The Paris Review*, previously of *SMTQ*, was hired as the workshop's director. I dropped out. I became an ascetic and gave all my money away to the poor. Then I wrote a book about asceticism, and the book sold so well, I made all my money back. Good timing; asceticism was in. I was prepared to do the same thing again, give my money away and then write about it, but then I got a letter informing me of Dingy the Pirate's death. At the funeral, I was shocked to see all my old twitter enemies (who now, by the way, constituted two-thirds of the teaching staff at the Iowa Writers' Workshop). They hated me more than ever because I was now a socialist: socialism was out. Apparently, Dingy had mentored all of them. This broke my heart. I thought my story was unique.

I gave all my money away again except for just enough to buy a small farm in Idaho, where I planned to write this book. One day, I went for a long walk. I got lost. As the sunlight faded, I stumbled into a clearing, where I saw a small farmhouse like mine. I knocked on the door. The man who answered looked familiar. Is it really you? I said. Yes, said Denis Johnson, I guess so. I told him my story, which was a story of loneliness and ostracization, the story of a true writer's life. Now that I was speaking to him face to face, in our own private Valhalla, it all seemed worth it. Before I could explain how much his writing had meant to me, he interrupted. Excuse me, he said, but can you please get off my farm? I'm pretty sick and I don't know who you are. I fell into a deep depression.

Somehow, I ended up in Myrtle Beach. I seem to remember sharing a motel room there with a strange bunch of evangelical Christians. They built bunk beds, triple-tiered, from scraps of wood found in the gutters of Kings Highway. They were always sniffing their own clothes. We ate government chicken straight from the microwave—the packaging said *government chicken*. I'd never seen anything like it. The walls seemed to be peeling. We all began to droop downward, our posture altered permanently by the monstrous humidity. They had developed something called the doctrine of divine nullification. It took me several weeks to get to the bottom of that phrase, over the course of which a number of the group's members disappeared, never to return. Those who remained never spoke of those who disappeared. Eventually, I realized they were killing themselves one by one. The doctrine of divine nullification suggested that if Jesus really was fully God (as well as fully man,) he must have committed suicide on the cross. Therefore, all true followers of Jesus must eventually, at the proper time, renounce the world via suicide. For them, the story of Jesus had become so much more real than their own lives that self-obliteration was the only prayer that made sense. Their necks had stiffened, they all had to turn at the waist to shift their field of vision, and my neck was stiffening too, and Jesus, I've got to get out of here, I thought, although I knew the truth, which was that I wouldn't kill myself. I think the humidity was driving me insane. Some of them could have been beautiful people, but they believed they had mastered the world, discovered its key, which made them absurd. One day, the absurd will be beautiful. But not yet. The older you get, the worse it seems to become, which is one of life's biggest surprises. One night, I rose from the place on the floor where I kept my pillow. Is it possible in humid climates for brain-altering parasites and amoebas to live in the air, poised, waiting for people to inhale? I settled into a deck chair by the abandoned motel pool. My heart began to race. I knew that eventually I would be the last man standing. The bunk beds would be mine. The room would be mine. I tried to remember their names, the names of the people killing themselves, but I kept coming up with the names of my twitter enemies instead, unless they all had the same names, which would be strange–

the kind of thing you only encounter in fables and folktales, parables and wild yarns, the world of coincidence, lies.

Thank you: Kevin Sampsell, Emma Alden, Minami Kobayashi, Anne Yoder, Woody Skinner, Andrea Vaughan, Mark Vaughan, Mom, Dad, Walker, Sylvie, and Rachel.

Thank you to the following websites and journals, where previous versions of stories in this book have appeared: *Always Crashing, Autofocus, Babel Tower Notice Board, Back Patio Press, Bluestem, HAD, Hobart, Miracle Monocle, Neutral Spaces Magazine, No Contact, Obliterat, Oyez Review, Words & Sports Quarterly,* and *X-R-A-Y.*

Note on the Author

Parker Young lives in Chicago with his family. This is his first book.